CHECKS AND BALANCES
IN THE U.S. GO

The U.S. Constitution
and the Separation of Powers

EDITED BY BRIAN DUIGNAN AND CAROLYN DECARLO

Britannica®
Educational Publishing

IN ASSOCIATION WITH

ROSEN
EDUCATIONAL SERVICES

Published in 2019 by Britannica Educational Publishing (a trademark of Encyclopædia Britannica, Inc.) in association with The Rosen Publishing Group, Inc. 29 East 21st Street, New York, NY 10010

Distributed exclusively by Rosen Publishing.
To see additional Britannica Educational Publishing titles, go to rosenpublishing.com.

Britannica Educational Publishing
J.E. Luebering: Executive Director, Core Editorial
Andrea R. Field: Managing Editor, Compton's by Britannica

Rosen Publishing
Carolyn DeCarlo: Editor
Nelson Sá: Art Director
Brian Garvey: Series Designer/Book Layout
Cindy Reiman: Photography Manager
Bruce Donnola: Photo Researcher

Cataloging-in-Publication Data

Names: Duignan, Brian, editor. | DeCarlo, Carolyn, editor.
Title: The U.S. Constitution and the separation of powers / edited by Brian Duignan and Carolyn DeCarlo.
Description: New York : Britannica Educational Publishing, in Association with Rosen Educational Services, 2019. | Series: Checks and balances in the U.S. government | Includes bibliographical references and index. | Audience: Grades 7-12.
Identifiers: ISBN 9781538301739 (library bound) | ISBN 9781538301746 (pbk.)
Subjects: LCSH: United States. Constitution—Juvenile literature. | Separation of powers—United States—Juvenile literature. | United States—Politics and government—Juvenile literature.
Classification: LCC E303.U836 2019 | DDC 342.7302'9--dc23

Manufactured in the United States of America

Photo credits: Cover, p. 1 Jeff Overs/BBC News & Current Affairs/Getty Images (document), Lightspring/Shutterstock.com (scale), © iStockphoto.com/arsenisspyros (capital); pp. 4-5, 113 © National Archives, Washington, D.C.; pp. 6-7 Hulton Archive/Archive Photos/Getty Images; pp. 13, 21 © Encyclopaedia Britannica, Inc.; pp. 24-25 © Comstock/Thinkstock; pp. 30, 67 Stock Montage/Archive Photos/Getty Images; p. 32 © Corbis; pp. 36-37 Robert W. Kelly/The Life Picture Collection/Getty Images; p. 38 © George Grantham Bain Collection/Library of Congress, Washington D.C. (digital file no. 19032); p. 41 © Harry S. Truman Library/NARA; p. 42 Mario Tama/Getty Images; p. 44 Paul Schutzer/The Life Picture Collection/Getty Images; pp. 45, 52, 54, 102 Bettmann/Getty Images; p. 47 Three Lions/Hulton Archive/Getty Images; pp. 56, 104, 111 © AP Images; p. 63 © The Federalist (vol.1) and A M'Lean, publisher, New York, 1788, from Rare Books and Special Collections Division in Madison's Treasures/Library of Congress, Washington, D.C.; p. 73 © Don Despain/MediaMagnet/SuperStock; p. 77 © Courtesy National Gallery of Art, Washington, D.C., Andrew W. Mellon Collection, 1942.8.34; p. 80 Laurence Saubadu/AFP/Newscom; p. 82 Thinkstock/Jupiter Images; p. 86 © Photos.com/Thinkstock; p. 92 Corbis Historical/Getty Images; p. 97 © Franz Jantzen/Supreme Court of the United States; p. 107 Hulton Deutsch/Corbis Historical/Getty Images.

CONTENTS

The U.S. Constitution, which provides the principles of government for the United States, is a landmark document of the Western world. It is the oldest written national constitution in use. Adopted in 1789, the Constitution divides governmental authority between a central national government and various separate state governments. It defined the principal organs of government and their jurisdictions as well as the basic rights of citizens, but it was not, however, the first such document created for the task in the United States. Its predecessor, the Articles of Confederation, was a kind of template for the Constitution, providing the new nation with its first, instructive experience in self-government under a written document.

The Articles of Confederation, in force from 1781 to 1789, served as a bridge between the early government

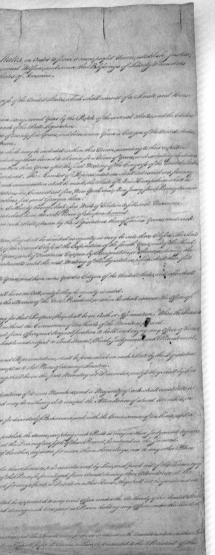

by the Continental Congress during the Revolutionary period and the federal system of government provided under the U.S. Constitution. Because the experience of overbearing British central authority was vivid in colonial minds, the drafters of the Articles deliberately established a confederation of sovereign states. Their intention is manifest in the name of the new nation, established in Article I: the United States of America. The Articles were written in 1776–77 and adopted by the Congress on November 15, 1777. However, the document was not fully ratified by the states until March 1, 1781.

On paper, the Congress had power to regulate foreign affairs, war, and the postal service and to appoint military officers, control Indian affairs, borrow and coin money, and issue bills of credit. In

An original copy of the U.S. Constitution is housed in the National Archives in Washington, D.C.

5

reality, however, the Articles gave the Congress no power to enforce its requests to the states for money or troops, and by the end of 1786 governmental effectiveness had broken down.

Nevertheless, some solid accomplishments had been achieved: certain state claims to western lands were settled, and the Northwest Ordinance of 1787 established the fundamental pattern of evolving government in the territories north of the Ohio River. Though on balance a flawed document, severely limiting the power of the central government, the short-lived Articles by their very weaknesses paved the way for the Constitutional Convention of 1787 and the present form of U.S. government.

The Constitution was written during the summer of 1787 in Philadelphia, Pennsylvania, by 55 delegates to a Constitutional Convention that was called ostensibly to amend the Articles of Confederation. The Constitution was the product of political compromise after long and often rancorous debates over issues such as states' rights, representation, and slavery. Delegates from

Future first President George Washington (1789–97) presides over the Constitutional Convention in Philadelphia, Pennsylvania, September 1787.

small and large states disagreed over whether the number of representatives in the new federal legislature should be the same for each state—as was the case under the Articles of Confederation—or different depending on a state's population. In addition, some delegates from Northern states sought to abolish slavery or, failing that, to make representation dependent on the size of a state's free population. At the same time, some Southern delegates threatened to abandon the convention if their demands to keep slavery and the slave trade legal and to count slaves for representation purposes were not met.

Eventually, the framers resolved their disputes by adopting a proposal put forward by the Connecticut delegation. The Great Compromise, as it came to be known, created a bicameral legislature with a Senate, in which all states would be equally represented, and a House of Representatives, in which representation would be apportioned on the basis of a state's free population plus three-fifths of its slave population. The new Constitution was submitted for ratification to the 13 states on September 28, 1787.

CHAPTER ONE

ARTICLES OF CONFEDERATION

The first constitution of the United States was known as the Articles of Confederation. The Articles were written in 1776–77, after independence from Great Britain had been declared and while the American Revolution was in progress. As a constitution, the Articles had a short life. The document was not fully ratified by the states until March 1, 1781, and it remained in effect only until March 4, 1789—the date on which the present U.S. Constitution went into effect. Under the Articles, Congress was the sole organ of government.

When the United States declared its independence in July 1776, the only institution acting as a central government was the Continental Congress. The states were operating under old colonial charters. Previously, the British Parliament had been the closest thing the colonies had to a national government. Thus, at the same time the united colonies were fighting to assure their independence, they were faced with the need to improvise a permanent national government and to formulate state constitutions.

THE FIRST STATE CONSTITUTIONS

To accomplish this, the states between 1777 and 1780 adopted written constitutions, or fundamental laws. The first of these were drawn up by the legislatures, but many believed that a constitution should not be made by the same method as that used in making ordinary laws. In Massachusetts, a constitution was rejected because it was prepared by the legislature. The state then called a special convention, the sole purpose of which was to frame a constitution. This set the fundamental law apart from acts of the legislature. Other states also followed this plan, which has become the typical American method.

In 1776, Americans were inclined to mistrust all government. Their troubles with England made them believe that officials who had much power would become unjust. To prevent this, seven states put into their new constitutions what were known as bills of rights. These listed many things that the government could not do. Among other things, it could not take a citizen's property without compensation, keep a citizen in prison without just cause, or deny a citizen the right of jury trial. The government was further limited by dividing its powers among the legislature, the executive, and the courts, so that each might act as a check on the others. If one department alone had all the power, it might use it unwisely or unfairly.

The patriot leaders remembered how the governors sent from England had generally acted contrary to the wishes of the people. For the most part, the new constitutions provided that the governor could not veto laws or dismiss the legislature, and they restricted his power to appoint local officers.

Democratic as they were in principle, the first state constitutions did not give all citizens equal political rights. In most states, less than half the men could vote, since there were fairly high property qualifications for voting and holding office and sometimes religious qualifications as well. Women were denied the right to vote, and slaves received no rights. The people of the seaboard obtained more delegates in the national legislature than did the poorer settlers of the interior. Yet the new governments were far more democratic than those immediately preceding: the governor was elected by the legislature or the voters; more people could vote, and the states did away with primogeniture—bestowing a landed estate on the oldest male heir by inheritance, leaving none to the other children.

The new constitutions were so well made that they lasted in many cases more than 40 years. They set in writing the rights for which English subjects had been fighting for centuries. They also preserved the institutions to which the Americans had grown accustomed: representation of the people, legislatures of two houses, town and county governments, and courts open to all.

THE NEED FOR A FEDERAL GOVERNMENT

At the same time, a plan for national government was being produced by members of the Second Continental Congress. On June 7, 1776—nearly a month before the Declaration of Independence was signed—delegate Richard Henry Lee of Virginia proposed that the Congress appoint a committee to draw up a plan of national government. The committee was composed of one delegate from each state. On July 12, it presented for approval a plan of union put together by John Dickinson of Pennsylvania.

Strong differences of opinion among the 13 states about a variety of issues kept debate on the document going for more than a year before the new constitution, or Articles of Confederation, was actually submitted to the states for approval. In addition, debate was delayed when the Congress was forced by events of the war to move its headquarters from Philadelphia to York, Pennsylvania, in 1777.

The first aim of the Articles was to give Congress the powers required for winning the war. But the citizens of the states knew that in time of peace they would have to continue working together. They would have to defend their frontiers and protect their trading vessels. They needed a common postal service and diplomatic agents abroad. The Articles created a perpetual union—not merely an alliance for war—and declared that the name of the nation should be The United States of America.

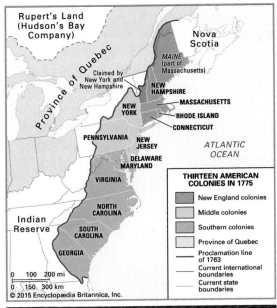

The 13 American colonies in 1775, with the Proclamation of 1763 boundary line, established by Great Britain to check new settlements by colonists on Native American land.

POWERS GRANTED TO CONGRESS

The main problem in drafting the Articles was that of dividing the powers of government between the states and Congress. England had formerly supplied the navy, the postal service, and the diplomatic agencies for America. It had also taken charge of the wars in which the colonies had participated. The patriots realized the value of having a single government do these things. Accordingly, the Articles gave Congress the power to raise and maintain an army and a navy, to make war and peace, to negotiate treaties, to fix standards of coinage and of weights and measures, and to provide a postal service.

On the other hand, the patriot leaders had objected to England's claim that Parliament could tax the colonies, regulate their trade, restrain them from issuing paper money, interfere in their local concerns, and take charge of relations with the American Indians. Therefore

EXCERPTS FROM ARTICLES OF CONFEDERATION

Articles of Confederation and Perpetual Union Between the States of New Hampshire, Massachusetts Bay, Rhode Island and Providence Plantations, Connecticut, New York, New Jersey, Pennsylvania, Delaware, Maryland, Virginia, North Carolina, South Carolina, and Georgia.

Article I. The style of this confederacy shall be "The United States of America."

Article II. Each state retains its sovereignty, freedom, and independence, and every power, jurisdiction, and right which is not by this confederation expressly delegated to the United States in Congress assembled.

Article III. The said states hereby severally enter into a firm league of friendship with each other, for their common defense, the security of their liberties, and their mutual and general welfare, binding themselves to assist each other against all force offered to, or attacks made upon them, or any of them, on account of religion, sovereignty, trade, or any other pretense whatever.

Article IV. The better to secure and perpetuate mutual friendship and intercourse among the people of the different states in this union, the free inhabitants of each of these states, paupers, vagabonds, and fugitives from justice excepted, shall be entitled to all privileges and immunities of free citizens in the several states. ...

Article V. For the more convenient management of the general interests of the United States, delegates shall be annually appointed in such manner as the legislature of each state shall direct, to meet in Congress on the first Monday in November, in every year. ...

No state shall be represented in Congress by less than two nor by more than seven members; and no person shall be capable of being a delegate for more than three years in any term of six years. ...

In determining questions in the United States in Congress assembled, each state shall have one vote. ...

Article VI. No state, without the consent of the United States in Congress assembled, shall send any embassy to, or receive any embassy from, or enter into any conference, agreement, alliance, or treaty with any king, prince, or state. ...

No state shall engage in any war without the consent of the United States in Congress assembled unless such state be actually invaded by enemies. ...

Article VII. When land forces are raised by any state for the common defense, all

(CONTINUED ON THE NEXT PAGE)

(CONTINUED FROM THE PREVIOUS PAGE)

officers of or under the rank of colonel shall be appointed by the legislature of each state respectively, by whom such forces shall be raised, or in such manner as such state shall direct. ...

Article VIII. All charges of war and all other expenses that shall be incurred for the common defense or general welfare, and allowed by the United States in Congress assembled, shall be defrayed out of a common treasury, which shall be supplied by the several states in proportion to the value of all land within each state. ...

Article IX. The United States in Congress assembled shall have the sole and exclusive right and power of determining on peace and war, except in the cases mentioned in the sixth article. ...

The United States in Congress assembled shall also have the sole and exclusive right and power of regulating the alloy and value of coin struck by their own authority or by that of the respective states ... regulating the trade and managing all affairs with the Indians not members of any of the states ... [and] establishing or regulating post offices from one state to another. ...

The United States in Congress assembled

shall have authority to appoint a committee, to sit in the recess of Congress, to be denominated "A Committee of the States," and to consist of one delegate from each state; ... to borrow money or emit bills on the credit of the United States ... to build and equip a navy — to agree upon the number of land forces, and to make requisitions from each state for its quota, in proportion to the number of white inhabitants in such state, which requisition shall be binding. ...

Article X. The Committee of the States, or any nine of them, shall be authorized to execute, in the recess of Congress, such of the powers of Congress as the United States in Congress assembled, by the consent of nine states, shall from time to time think expedient to vest them with. ...

Article XI. Canada acceding to this Confederation, and joining in the measures of the United States, shall be admitted into and entitled to all the advantages of this union; but no other colony shall be admitted into the same unless such admission be agreed to by nine states.

Article XII. All bills of credit emitted, moneys borrowed, and debts contracted by or under the authority of Congress, before the assembling of the United States, in pursuance of the present Confederation,

(CONTINUED ON THE NEXT PAGE)

(CONTINUED FROM THE PREVIOUS PAGE)

shall be deemed and considered as a charge against the United States, for payment and satisfaction whereof the said United States and the public faith are hereby solemnly pledged.

Article XIII. Every state shall abide by the determinations of the United States in Congress assembled on all questions which by this Confederation are submitted to them. And the Articles of this Confederation shall be inviolably observed by every state, and the union shall be perpetual; nor shall any alteration at any time hereafter be made in any of them; unless such alteration be agreed to in a Congress of the United States and be afterward confirmed by the legislatures of every state.

the Articles did not allow Congress any control over the domestic affairs of the states. Nor could it levy taxes; it could only ask the states for funds. Congress could make commercial treaties and also superintend Indian affairs so far as its acts did not conflict with state laws.

Each of the 13 states was to have only one vote in Congress, though it might send from two to seven delegates, and nine of the 13 votes were required before Congress could act. The enforcement of all laws and the administration of justice were left to the states. The Articles could be changed only by unanimous vote of the Confederation. Any power not specifically granted to Congress was reserved to the states.

ADVANTAGES AND WEAKNESSES OF UNION

The Articles were adopted by Congress on November 15, 1777, and submitted to the states for ratification. The smaller states, especially Maryland, objected to the claims of Virginia, Massachusetts, the Carolinas, Georgia, New York, and Connecticut to the lands west of the Appalachians. Maryland felt that if these states had all the western land they claimed, they might become overwhelmingly powerful. Only when the states with western land claims agreed to turn over these lands to Congress for the use of all the states would Maryland ratify the Articles. It finally signed them on March 1, 1781.

Thus the Articles, which had been laid before the states in 1777 and which were intended to help win the war, did not come into effect until a few months before the close of the war. The new Congress had only to keep the armies in the field until the war was won. It provided four executive offices to superintend foreign affairs, finance, war, and marine. Through the efforts of the able superintendent of finance, Robert Morris, money was borrowed from Holland and France, and further sums were obtained from the states. Congress also negotiated the peace treaty that secured independence and granted the new country the land west to the Mississippi River.

Congress worked out important policies with reference to the western lands ceded by the states. An Ordinance of 1785 provided for dividing these lands into townships of 36 square miles (93 square kilometres) and allowed the sale of 640-acre (258-hectare) tracts at about a dollar an acre. Many settlers were able to buy farms of their own. The Ordinance of 1787, also known as the Northwest Ordinance, opened the territory to settlement and outlined the representative government later used for all the continental territories. It promised that the region should eventually be divided into new states that would enter the Union on an equal footing with the original 13.

After the war, the states refused to pay taxes requested by Congress; hence the general government could not pay the public debt or even the interest on it. The Navy was inadequate to protect foreign commerce. Now that the states were out of the British Empire, they were not allowed to trade freely with England and its West Indies colonies. The settlers in the West needed an outlet for their produce down the Mississippi. Spain, however, held the mouth of the river and refused to allow them to ship their products from New Orleans. Congress found that it could not get commercial favours from either England or Spain. Since the states had the final say in commercial regulations, a treaty of Congress had little force and the

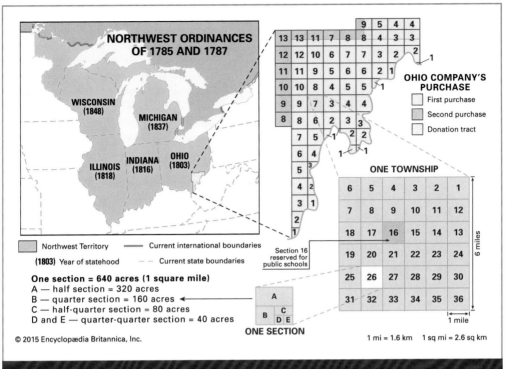

NORTHWEST ORDINANCES OF 1785 AND 1787

WISCONSIN (1848)

MICHIGAN (1837)

ILLINOIS (1818) INDIANA (1816) OHIO (1803)

OHIO COMPANY'S PURCHASE
First purchase
Second purchase
Donation tract

ONE TOWNSHIP

6	5	4	3	2	1
7	8	9	10	11	12
18	17	16	15	14	13
19	20	21	22	23	24
25	26	27	28	29	30
31	32	33	34	35	36

6 miles

1 mile

Section 16 reserved for public schools

Northwest Territory
(1803) Year of statehood
Current international boundaries
Current state boundaries

One section = 640 acres (1 square mile)
A — half section = 320 acres
B — quarter section = 160 acres
C — half-quarter section = 80 acres
D and E — quarter-quarter section = 40 acres

ONE SECTION

1 mi = 1.6 km   1 sq mi = 2.6 sq km

© 2015 Encyclopædia Britannica, Inc.

The Northwest Territory was created by the Northwest Ordinances of 1785 and 1787, with the Ohio Company of Associates' purchase (ca. 1787) and township schemes.

European countries preferred to deal separately with the states.

After the American Revolution, a period of hard times set in. The price of farm products was very low, and the farmers bought manufactured goods on credit. Then they found great difficulty in paying their debts. They soon asked their legislatures to issue paper money that creditors would have to accept. Massachusetts experienced a violent struggle between the debtor farmers and their creditors known as Shays's Rebellion. Congress, however, could not prevent the states from issuing cheap paper money or act to put down a civil war.

The first Union allowed people to move freely throughout the country. The Congress, however, could not enforce a law or collect a tax. It had no power to control foreign trade, or to restrain the states from trade wars among themselves. And there was neither an executive to carry out the acts of Congress nor a federal court to interpret and enforce the laws. The Union under the Articles, however, carried the United States through a critical period and paved the way for the "more perfect union" of the Constitution.

CHAPTER TWO

FRAMING THE CONSTITUTION

In 1787–88, in an effort to persuade New York to ratify the Constitution, Alexander Hamilton, John Jay, and James Madison published a series of essays on the Constitution and republican government in New York newspapers. Their work, written under the pseudonym "Publius" and collected and published in book form as *The Federalist* (1788), became a classic exposition and defense of the Constitution.

In June 1788, after the Constitution had been ratified by nine states (as required by Article VII), Congress set March 4, 1789, as the date for the new government to commence proceedings (the first elections under the Constitution were held late in 1788). Because ratification in many states was contingent on the promised addition of a Bill of Rights, Congress proposed 12 amendments in September 1789; 10 were ratified by the states, and their adoption was certified on December 15, 1791. (One of the original 12 proposed amendments, which prohibited mid-term changes in compensation for members of Congress, was ratified in 1992 as the Twenty-seventh Amendment.

The last one, concerning the ratio of citizens per member of the House of Representatives, has never been adopted.)

ARTICLES OF THE CONSTITUTION

The authors of the Constitution were heavily influenced by the country's experience under the Articles of Confederation, which had attempted to retain as much independence and sovereignty for the states as possible and to assign to the central government only those nationally important functions that the states could not handle individually. But the events of the years 1781 to 1787, including the national government's inability to act during Shays's Rebellion (1786–87) in Massachusetts, showed that the Articles were unworkable because they deprived the national government of many essential powers, including direct taxation and the ability to regulate interstate commerce. It was hoped that the new Constitution would remedy this problem.

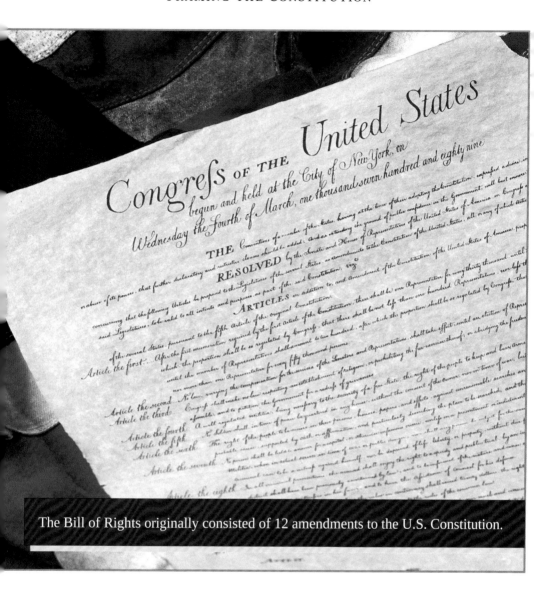

The Bill of Rights originally consisted of 12 amendments to the U.S. Constitution.

The framers of the Constitution were especially concerned with limiting the power of government and securing the liberty of citizens. The doctrine of legislative, executive, and judicial separation of powers, the checks and balances of each branch against the others, and the explicit guarantees of individual liberty were all designed to strike a balance between authority and liberty—the central purpose of American constitutional law.

ARTICLE I

With this purpose in mind, the Constitution concisely organizes the country's basic political institutions. The main text comprises seven articles. Article I vests all legislative powers in the Congress—the House of Representatives and the Senate. The Great Compromise stipulated that representation in the House would be based on population, and each state is entitled to two senators. Members of the House serve terms of two years, senators terms of six. Among the powers delegated to Congress are the right to levy taxes, borrow money, regulate interstate commerce, provide for military forces, declare war, and determine member seating and rules of procedure. The House initiates impeachment proceedings, and the Senate adjudicates them.

ARTICLE II

Article II vests executive power in the office of the presidency of the United States. The president, selected by an electoral college to serve a four-year term, is given responsibilities common to chief executives, including serving as commander in chief of the armed forces, negotiating treaties (when supported by two-thirds of the Senate), and granting pardons. The president's vast appointment powers, which include members of the Federal Judiciary and the cabinet, are subject to the "advice and consent" two-thirds(majority approval) of the Senate (Article II, Section 2). Originally presidents were eligible for continual reelection, but the Twenty-second Amendment (1951) later prohibited any person from being elected president more than twice. Although the formal powers of the president are constitutionally quite limited and vague in comparison with those of the Congress, a variety of historical and technological factors—such as the centralization of power in the executive branch during war and the advent of television—have increased the informal responsibilities of the office extensively to embrace other aspects of political leadership, including proposing legislation to Congress.

ARTICLE III

Article III places judicial power in the hands of the courts. The Constitution is interpreted by the courts, and the Supreme Court of the United States is the final court of appeal from the state and lower federal courts. The power of American courts to rule on the constitutionality of laws, known as judicial review, is held by few other courts in the world and is not explicitly granted in the Constitution. The principle of judicial review was first asserted by

THE CONSTITUTION OF THE UNITED STATES: ARTICLE III, SECTIONS 1 AND 2

Section 1. The judicial power of the United States shall be vested in one Supreme Court, and in such inferior courts as the Congress may from time to time ordain and establish. The judges, both of the Supreme and inferior courts, shall hold their offices during good behavior, and shall, at stated times, receive for their services a compensation which shall not be diminished during their continuance in office.

Section 2. The judicial power shall extend to all cases, in law and equity, arising under this Constitution, the laws of the United States, and treaties made, or which shall be made, under their authority; to all cases affecting ambassadors, other public ministers and consuls; to all cases of Admiralty and maritime jurisdiction; to controversies to which the United States shall be a party; to controversies between two or more states; between a state and citizens of another state; between citizens of different states; between citizens of the same state claiming lands under grants of different states; and between a state, or the citizens thereof, and foreign states, citizens, or subjects.

In all cases affecting ambassadors, other public ministers, and consuls, and those in which a state shall be party, the Supreme Court shall have original jurisdiction. In all the other cases beforementioned, the Supreme Court shall have appellate jurisdiction, both as to law and fact, with such exceptions and under such regulations as the Congress shall make.

The trial of all crimes, except in cases of impeachment, shall be by jury; and such trial shall be held in the state where the said crimes shall have been committed; but when not committed within any state, the trial shall be at such place or places as the Congress may be law have directed.

Supreme Court Chief Justice John Marshall in *Marbury v. Madison* (1803), when the court ruled that it had the authority to void national or state laws.

Beyond the body of judicial rulings interpreting it, the Constitution acquires meaning in a broader sense

Chief Justice of the Supreme Court John Marshall (served 1801–1835).

at the hands of all who use it. Congress on innumerable occasions has given new scope to the document through statutes, such as those creating executive departments, the federal courts, territories, and states; controlling succession to the presidency; and setting up the executive budget system. The chief executive also has contributed to constitutional interpretation, as in the development of the executive agreement as an instrument of foreign policy. Practices outside the letter of the Constitution based on custom and usage are often recognized as constitutional elements; they include the system of political parties, presidential nomination procedures, and the conduct of election campaigns. The presidential cabinet is largely a constitutional "convention" based on custom, and the actual operation of the electoral college system is also a convention.

ARTICLE IV

Article IV deals, in part, with relations between the states and privileges of the citizens of the states. These provisions include the full faith and credit clause, which requires states to recognize the official acts and judicial proceedings of other states; the requirement that each state provide citizens from other states with all the privileges and immunities afforded the citizens of that state; and the guarantee of a republican form of government for each state.

ARTICLE V

Article V stipulates the procedures for amending the Constitution. Amendments may be proposed by a two-thirds vote of both houses of Congress or by a convention called by Congress on the application of the legislatures of two-thirds of the states. Proposed amendments must be ratified by three-fourths of the state legislatures or by conventions in as many states, depending on the decision of Congress. All subsequent amendments have been proposed by Congress, and all but one—the Twenty-first Amendment, which repealed prohibition—have been ratified by state legislatures.

United States Capitol, Washington, D.C., the meeting place of the U.S. Congress.

ARTICLES VI AND VII

Article VI, which prohibits religious tests for office-holders, also deals with public debts and the supremacy of the Constitution, citing the document as "the supreme Law of the Land; . . . any Thing in the Constitution or Laws of any State to the Contrary notwithstanding." Article VII stipulated that the Constitution would become operational after being ratified by nine states.

The national government has only those constitutional powers that are delegated to it either expressly or by implication; the states, unless otherwise restricted, possess all the remaining powers (Tenth Amendment). Thus, national powers are enumerated (Article I, Section 8, paragraphs 1–17), and state powers are not. The state powers are often called "residual," or "reserved," powers. The elastic, or necessary and proper, clause (Article I, Section 8, paragraph 18) states that Congress shall have the authority "To make all Laws which shall be necessary and proper for carrying into Execution" the various powers vested in the national government. Thus, it follows that, in addition to the delegated powers, Congress possesses "implied" powers, a proposition established by Chief Justice Marshall in *McCulloch* v. *Maryland* (1819). The issue of national versus state power was not fully resolved by this decision, however.

MCCULLOCH v. MARYLAND

On March 6, 1819, in *McCulloch v. Maryland*, the U.S. Supreme Court affirmed the constitutional doctrine of Congress's "implied powers." It determined that Congress had not only the powers expressly conferred upon it by the Constitution but also all authority "appropriate" to carry out such powers. In the specific case the court held that Congress had the power to incorporate a national bank, despite the Constitution's silence on both the creation of corporations and the chartering of banks. It was concluded that since a national bank would facilitate the accomplishment of purposes expressly confided to the federal government, such as the collection of taxes and the maintenance of armed forces, Congress had a choice of means to achieve these proper ends. The doctrine of implied powers became a powerful force in the steady growth of federal power.

Competing concepts of federal supremacy and states' rights were brought into sharp relief in questions about commercial regulation. The commerce clause simply authorized Congress "to regulate Commerce with foreign Nations, and among the several

States, and with the Indian Tribes." Particularly since a series of decisions in 1937, the court has interpreted Congress's regulatory power broadly under the commerce clause as new methods of interstate transportation and communication have come into use. States may not regulate any aspect of interstate commerce that Congress has preempted.

CIVIL LIBERTIES AND THE BILL OF RIGHTS

The federal government is obliged by many constitutional provisions to respect the individual citizen's basic rights. Some civil liberties were specified in the original document, notably in the provisions guaranteeing the writ of habeas corpus and trial by jury in criminal cases (Article III, Section 2) and forbidding bills of attainder and ex post facto laws (Article I, Section 9). But the most significant limitations to government's power over the individual were added in 1791 in the Bill of Rights.

The Constitution's First Amendment guarantees the rights of conscience, such as freedom of religion, speech, and the press, and the right of peaceful assembly and petition. Other guarantees in the Bill of Rights require fair procedures for persons accused of a crime—such as protection against unreasonable search and seizure, compulsory self-incrimination, double jeopardy, and excessive bail—and guarantees of a speedy and public trial by a local,

A massive crowd assembles on the National Mall in front of the reflecting pool during the civil rights March on Washington for Jobs and Freedom, August 28, 1963. Here, Martin Luther King, Jr., gave his "I Have a Dream" speech.

impartial jury before an impartial judge and representation by counsel. Rights of private property are also guaranteed.

Although the Bill of Rights is a broad expression of individual civil liberties, the ambiguous wording of many of its provisions—such as the Second Amendment's right "to keep and bear arms" and the Eighth Amendment's prohibition of "cruel and unusual punishments"—has been a source of constitutional controversy and intense political debate. Further, the rights guaranteed are not absolute, and there has been considerable disagreement about the extent to which they limit governmental authority. The Bill of Rights originally protected citizens only from the national government. For example, although the Constitution prohibited the establishment of an official religion at the national level, the official state-supported religion of Massachusetts was Congregationalism until 1833. Thus, individual citizens had to look to state constitutions for protection of their rights against state governments.

AMENDMENTS SINCE THE BILL OF RIGHTS

Twenty-seven amendments have been added to the Constitution since 1789, seventeen since the first ten were passed as the Bill of Rights. In addition to those mentioned above, other far-reaching amendments include the Sixteenth (1913), which allowed Congress to impose an income tax; the Seventeenth (1913), which provided for direct election of senators; the Nineteenth (1920), which mandated woman suffrage; and the Twenty-sixth (1971), which granted suffrage to citizens 18 years of age and older.

Woman suffrage advocates parade in an open car in support of ratification of the Nineteenth Amendment to the U.S. Constitution, which granted women the right to vote in federal elections.

In more than two centuries of operation, the United States Constitution has proved itself a dynamic document. It has served as a model for other countries, its provisions being widely imitated in national constitutions throughout the world. Although the Constitution's brevity and ambiguity have sometimes led to serious disputes about its meaning, they also have made it adaptable to changing historical circumstances and ensured its relevance in ages far removed from the one in which it was written.

CHAPTER THREE

Equal Protection Comes of Age

The civil rights movement in the United States that blossomed in the late 1950s applied nonviolent protest action to break the pattern of racially segregated public facilities in the South and eventually to achieve passage of the comprehensive Civil Rights Act (1964).

Denied constitutional guarantees (1787) because of their mainly slave status at the founding of the republic, African Americans were first promised fundamental citizenship rights in the Thirteenth through Fifteenth constitutional amendments (1865–70). The Thirteenth abolished slavery; the Fourteenth granted citizenship to former slaves; and the Fifteenth guaranteed former male slaves the right to vote. The Fourteenth Amendment placed an important federal limitation on the states by forbidding them to deny to any person "life, liberty, or property, without due process of law" and guaranteeing every person within a state's jurisdiction "the equal protection of its laws." Later interpretations by the Supreme Court in the

20th century gave these two clauses added significance. Most controversial was the Supreme Court's application of this due process clause to the *Roe* v. *Wade* case, which led to the legalization of abortion in 1973.

The Civil Rights Act of 1875 required equal accommodations for blacks and whites in public facilities (other than schools), but this legislation was effectively voided by the Supreme Court in 1883. By 1900, 18 states of the North and West had legislated public policies against racial discrimination, but in the South new Jim Crow laws eroded the franchise and reinforced segregation practices, while the U.S. Supreme Court's decision in *Plessy* v. *Ferguson* (1896) legitimized the segregation of blacks from whites.

THE CIVIL RIGHTS MOVEMENT

During World War II, progress was made in outlawing discrimination in defense industries (1941) and after the war in desegregating the armed forces (1948). During the late

Harry Truman shakes hands with troops in 1947.

1940s and early 1950s, lawyers for the National Association for the Advancement of Colored People (NAACP) pressed a series of important cases before the Supreme Court in which they argued that segregation meant inherently unequal (and inadequate) educational and other public facilities for African Americans. These cases culminated in the Court's landmark decision in *Brown* v. *Board of Education of Topeka* (May 17, 1954). This historic decision was to stimulate a mass movement on the part of African Americans and white sympathizers to try to end the segregationist practices and racial inequalities that were firmly entrenched across the nation and particularly in the South. The movement was strongly resisted by many whites in the South and elsewhere.

Members of the class of 2007 celebrate their graduation from John McDonogh Senior High School, a predominantly African American inner city school in New Orleans. Decades after the *Brown* decision, many American schools are effectively segregated because of where people live.

After an African American woman, Rosa Parks, was arrested for refusing to move to the black section of a bus in Montgomery, Alabama (December 1, 1955), African Americans staged a one-day local boycott of the bus system to protest her arrest. Fusing these protest elements with the historic force of African American churches, a local Baptist minister, Martin Luther King, Jr., succeeded in transforming a spontaneous racial protest into a massive resistance movement, led from 1957 by his Southern Christian Leadership Conference (SCLC). After a protracted boycott of the Montgomery bus company forced it to desegregate its facilities, picketing and boycotting spread rapidly to other communities. During the period from 1955 to 1960, some progress was made toward integrating schools and other public facilities in the upper South and the border states, but the Deep South remained adamant in its opposition to most desegregation measures.

In 1960 the sit-in movement (largely under the auspices of the newly formed Student Nonviolent Coordinating Committee; SNCC) was launched in Greensboro, North Carolina, when African American college students insisted on service at a local segregated lunch counter. Patterning its techniques on the nonviolent methods of Indian leader Mohandas Gandhi, the movement spread across the nation, forcing the desegregation of department stores, supermarkets, libraries, and movie theatres. In May 1961, the Congress of Racial Equality (CORE) sent Freedom Riders of both races through the South and elsewhere

A group of Freedom Riders stand in line, May 1961.

to test and break down segregated accommodations in interstate transportation. By September it was estimated that more than 70,000 students had participated in the movement, with approximately 3,600 arrested; more than 100 cities in 20 states had been affected. The movement reached its climax in August 1963 with the massive March on Washington, D.C., to protest racial discrimination and demonstrate support for major civil rights legislation that was pending in Congress.

The federal government under presidents Dwight D. Eisenhower (1953–61) and John F. Kennedy had been reluctant to vigorously enforce the *Brown* decision when this entailed directly confronting the resistance of Southern whites. In 1961–63 President Kennedy won a following in the African American community by encouraging the movement's leaders, but Kennedy's administration lacked the political capacity to persuade Congress to pass new legislation guaranteeing integration and equal rights. After Kennedy's assassination (November 1963), Congress, under the prodding of President Lyndon B. Johnson, in 1964 passed the Civil Rights Act. This was the most far-reaching civil rights bill in the nation's history (indeed, in world history), forbidding discrimination in public accommodations and threatening to withhold federal funds from

Civil rights supporters, including (*from left*) Hubert Humphrey, Ralph Abernathy, and Martin Luther King, Jr., hold their fingers in a victory salute on March 26, 1964.

THE EQUAL EMPLOYMENT OPPORTUNITY COMMISSION

The Equal Employment Opportunity Commission (EEOC) is a government agency established on July 2, 1965, by Title VII of the Civil Rights Act of 1964 to "ensure equality of opportunity by vigorously enforcing federal legislation prohibiting discrimination in employment"—particularly discrimination on the basis of religion, race, sex, colour, national origin, age, or disability. The EEOC investigates claims of discrimination on the federal level and attempts mediation. If mediation is impossible, the EEOC will bring a suit against the offending company. The agency also works with fair employment practice agencies at the state and local level. In 1991 the EEOC further expanded to include several educational and technical assistance programs to further equal employment practices. The EEOC and its field offices manage thousands of claims of employment discrimination annually.

communities that persisted in maintaining segregated schools. It was followed in 1965 by the passage of the Voting Rights Act, the enforcement of which eradicated the tactics previously used in the South to disenfranchise

African American voters. This act led to drastic increases in the numbers of African American registered voters in the South, with a comparable increase in the numbers of African Americans holding elective offices there.

Up until 1966 the civil rights movement had united widely disparate elements in the black community along with their white supporters and sympathizers, but in that year signs of radicalism began to appear in the movement as younger African Americans became impatient with

African American leader Malcolm X advocated a more radical approach to achieving civil rights than his contemporary Martin Luther King, Jr.

the rate of change and dissatisfied with purely nonviolent methods of protest. This new militancy split the ranks of the movement's leaders and also alienated some white sympathizers, a process that was accelerated by a wave of rioting in the African American ghettos of several major cities in 1965–67. After the assassination of King (April 1968) and further rioting in the cities, the movement as a cohesive effort disintegrated, with a broad spectrum of leadership advocating different approaches and varying degrees of militancy.

In the decades that followed, many civil rights leaders sought to achieve greater direct political power through elective office, and they sought to achieve more substantive economic and educational gains through affirmative-action programs that compensated for past discrimination in job hiring and college admissions. Although the civil rights movement was less militant, it was persevering.

EQUAL PROTECTION

Equal protection is the constitutional guarantee in the United States that no person or group will be denied the protection under the law that is enjoyed by similar persons or groups. In other words, persons similarly situated must be similarly treated. Equal protection is extended when the rules of law are applied equally in all like cases and when persons are exempt from obligations greater than those imposed upon others in like circumstances. The Fourteenth Amendment to the U.S. Constitution, one of three amendments adopted in the immediate aftermath of the American Civil War (1861–65), prohibits states from denying to any person "the equal protection of the laws."

For much of the post–Civil War period, the Supreme Court held that the postwar amendments had but one purpose: to guarantee "the freedom of the slave race . . . and the protection of the newly-made freeman and citizen from the oppressions of those who had formerly exercised unlimited domination over him."

Thus, the equal-protection clause of the Fourteenth Amendment was applied minimally—except in some cases of racial discrimination, such as the invalidation of literacy tests and grandfather clauses for voting. In other decisions—such as *Plessy* (1896) and the decisions creating

THE FOURTEENTH AMENDMENT

[1868] Section 1—All persons born or naturalized in the United States, and subject to the jurisdiction thereof, are citizens of the United States and of the State

(CONTINUED ON THE NEXT PAGE)

(CONTINUED FROM THE PREVIOUS PAGE)

wherein they reside. No State shall make or enforce any law which shall abridge the privileges or immunities of citizens of the United States; nor shall any State deprive any person of life, liberty, or property, without due process of law; nor deny to any person within its jurisdiction the equal protection of the laws.

Section 2—Representatives shall be apportioned among the several States according to their respective numbers, counting the whole number of persons in each State, excluding Indians not taxed. But when the right to vote at any election for the choice of electors for President and Vice President of the United States, Representatives in Congress, the Executive and Judicial officers of a State, or the members of the Legislature thereof, is denied to any of the male inhabitants of such State, being twenty-one years of age, and citizens of the United States, or in any way abridged, except for participation in rebellion, or other crime, the basis of representation therein shall be reduced in the proportion which the number of such male citizens shall bear to the whole number of male citizens twenty-one years of age in such State.

Section 3—No person shall be a Senator

or Representative in Congress, or elector of President and Vice President, or hold any office, civil or military, under the United States, or under any State, who, having previously taken an oath, as a member of Congress, or as an officer of the United States, or as a member of any State legislature, or as an executive or judicial officer of any State, to support the Constitution of the United States, shall have engaged in insurrection or rebellion against the same, or given aid or comfort to the enemies thereof. But Congress may by a vote of two-thirds of each House, remove such disability.

Section 4—The validity of the public debt of the United States, authorized by law, including debts incurred for payment of pensions and bounties for services in suppressing insurrection or rebellion, shall not be questioned. But neither the United States nor any State shall assume or pay any debt or obligation incurred in aid of insurrection or rebellion against the United States, or any claim for the loss or emancipation of any slave; but all such debts, obligations and claims shall be held illegal and void.

Section 5—The Congress shall have power to enforce, by appropriate legislation, the provisions of this article.

the doctrine of state action, which limited the enforcement of national civil rights legislation—the court diminished the envisioned protections. Indeed, for nearly eighty years after the adoption of the Fourteenth Amendment, the intent of the equal-protection clause was effectively circumvented. As late as 1927, Justice Oliver Wendell Holmes, Jr., referred to equal protection as "the usual last resort of constitutional arguments." Not until the landmark *Brown* v. *Board of Education* (1954) decision did the court reverse its decision in *Plessy*.

Under Chief Justice Earl Warren in the 1960s, the concept of equal protection was dramatically transformed and applied to cases involving welfare benefits, exclusionary zoning, municipal services, and school financing. Equal protection became a prolific source of constitutional litigation. During the tenure of Chief Justices Warren E. Burger and William H. Rehnquist, the court added considerably to the list of

Chief Justice Earl Warren.

situations that might be adjudicated under the doctrine of equal protection, including sexual discrimination, the status and rights of aliens, voting, abortion, and access to the courts. In *Bush* v. *Gore* (2000), which stemmed from the controversial presidential election of that year, the Supreme Court's ruling that a selective recount of ballots in the state of Florida violated the equal-protection clause helped to preserve George W. Bush's narrow win in that state and in the electoral college.

THE VOTING RIGHTS ACT

The Voting Rights Act was adopted on August 6, 1965, and aimed to overcome legal barriers at the state and local levels that prevented African Americans from exercising their right to vote under the U.S. Constitution's Fifteenth Amendment (1870). The act significantly widened the franchise and is considered among the most far-reaching pieces of civil rights legislation in U.S. history.

Shortly following the end of the Civil War in 1865, the Fifteenth Amendment was ratified, guaranteeing that the right to vote would not be denied "on account of race, color, or previous condition of servitude." Soon afterward, the U.S. Congress enacted legislation that made it a federal crime to interfere with an individual's right to vote and that otherwise protected the rights promised to former slaves under both the Fourteenth (1868) and Fifteenth amendments. In some states of the former Confederacy, African

Prospective African American voters register to exercise their rights under the Fifteenth Amendment in the basement of a U.S. post office in Mississippi, August 1965.

Americans became a majority or near majority of the eligible voting population, and African American candidates ran and were elected to office at all levels of government.

Nevertheless, there was strong opposition to the extension of the franchise to African Americans. Following the end of Reconstruction, the Supreme Court of the United States limited voting protections under federal legislation, and intimidation and fraud were employed by white leaders to reduce voter registration and turnout among African Americans. As whites came to dominate state legislatures once again, legislation was used to strictly circumscribe the right of African Americans to vote. Poll taxes, literacy tests, grandfather clauses, whites-only primaries, and other measures disproportionately disqualified African Americans from voting. The result was that by the early 20th century nearly all African Americans were disfranchised. In the first half of the 20th century, several such measures were declared unconstitutional by the U.S. Supreme Court. In 1915, for example, grandfather clauses were invalidated, and in 1944 whites-only primaries were struck down. Nevertheless, by the early 1960s voter registration rates among African Americans were negligible in much of the Deep South and well below those of whites elsewhere.

In the 1950s and early 1960s the U.S. Congress enacted laws to protect the right of African Americans to vote, but such legislation was only partially successful. In 1964 the Civil Rights Act was passed and the Twenty-fourth Amendment, abolishing poll taxes for voting for federal offices, was ratified, and the following year President Lyndon B. Johnson called for the implementation of comprehensive federal legislation to protect voting rights. The resulting act, the Voting Rights Act, suspended literacy tests, provided for federal approval of proposed changes to voting laws or procedures ("preclearance") in areas that had previously used tests to determine voter eligibility (these areas were covered under Sections 4 and 5 of the legislation), and directed the attorney general of the United States to challenge the use of poll taxes for state and local elections. An expansion of the law in the 1970s also protected voting rights for non-English-speaking U.S. citizens. Sections 4 and 5 were extended for five years in 1970, seven years in 1975, and 25 years in both 1982 and 2006.

The Voting Rights Act resulted in a marked decrease in the voter registration disparity between whites and blacks. In the mid-1960s, for example, the overall proportion of white to black registration in the South ranged from about 2 to 1 to 3 to 1 (and about 10 to 1 in Mississippi); by the late 1980s racial variations in voter registration had largely disappeared. As the number of African American voters increased, so did the number of African American elected officials. In the mid-1960s there were about 70 African American elected officials in the South, but by the turn of the 21st century there were some 5,000, and the

Members of the Congressional Black Caucus stand beside Representative James Clyburn during a news conference on Capitol Hill, December 5, 2000.

number of African American members of the U.S. Congress had increased from 6 to about 40. In what was widely perceived as a test case, *Northwest Austin Municipal Utility District Number One* v. *Holder, et al.* (2009), the Supreme Court declined to rule on the constitutionality of the Voting Rights Act. In *Shelby County* v. *Holder* (2013), however, the court struck down Section 4—which had established a formula for identifying jurisdictions that were required to obtain preclearance—declaring it to be unjustified in light of changed historical circumstances. As a result, Section 5 became unenforceable, and many states that had previously been subject to preclearance began to pass strict voter ID laws, which disproportionally affected black and minority voters.

CHAPTER FOUR

EQUALIZING MEASURES

The Constitution created three separate branches of government (executive, judicial, and legislative) and a system whereby each branch could check and balance the power of the other two. In a series of essays collectively known as the Federalist Papers, Alexander Hamilton, James Madison, and John Jay argued persuasively that such a federal system would be best equipped to protect the rights of individuals while also providing for justice and the general welfare.

SEPARATION OF POWERS

Separation of powers is the division of the legislative, executive, and judicial functions of government among separate and independent bodies. Such a separation, it has been argued, limits the possibility of arbitrary excesses by government, since the sanction of all three branches is required for the making, executing, and administering of laws.

The doctrine may be traced to ancient and medieval theories of mixed government, which argued that the processes of government should involve the different elements in society such as monarchic, aristocratic, and democratic interests. The first modern formulation of the doctrine was that of the French writer Montesquieu in *The Spirit of Laws* (1748), although the English philosopher John Locke had earlier argued that legislative power should be divided between king and Parliament.

Montesquieu's argument that liberty is most effectively safeguarded by the separation of powers was inspired by the English constitution, although his interpretation of English political realities has since been disputed. His work was widely influential, most notably in America, where it profoundly influenced the framing of the Constitution. The U.S. Constitution further precluded the concentration of political power by providing staggered terms of office in the key governmental bodies.

Modern constitutional systems show a great variety of arrangements of the legislative, executive, and judicial processes, and the doctrine has consequently lost much of its rigidity and dogmatic purity. In the 20th century, and especially since World War II, governmental involvement in numerous aspects of social and economic life has resulted in an enlargement of the scope of executive power. Some who fear the consequences of this for individual liberty have favoured establishing means of appeal against executive and administrative decisions (for example, through an ombudsman), rather than attempting to reassert the doctrine of the separation of powers.

CHECKS AND BALANCES

Checks and balances is a principle of government under which separate branches are empowered to prevent actions by other branches and are induced to share power. It is applied primarily in constitutional governments and is of fundamental importance in tripartite governments, such as that of the United States, which divide powers among legislative, executive, and judicial branches.

The framers of the U.S. Constitution, who were influenced by Montesquieu and the English jurist and common-law scholar William Blackstone, among others, saw checks and balances as essential for securing liberty under the Constitution: "It is by balancing each of these powers against the other two, that the efforts in human nature toward tyranny can alone be checked and restrained, and any degree of freedom preserved in the constitution" (John Adams). Though not expressly covered in the text of the Constitution, judicial review—the power of the courts to examine the actions of the legislative and the executive arms of government to ensure that they are constitutional—became an important part of government in the United States. Other checks and balances include the presidential veto of legislation (which Congress may override by a two-thirds vote) and executive and judicial impeachment by Congress. Only Congress can appropriate funds, and each house serves as a check on possible abuses of power or unwise action by the other. Congress, by initiating constitutional amendments, can reverse decisions of the Supreme Court. The president appoints the members of the Supreme Court but only with the consent of the Senate, which also approves certain other executive appointments. The Senate also must approve treaties.

From 1932, the U.S. Congress exercised a so-called legislative veto. Clauses in certain laws qualified the authority of the executive branch to act by making specified acts subject to disapproval by the majority vote of one or both houses. In 1983, in a case concerning the deportation of an alien, the U.S. Supreme Court held that legislative vetoes were unconstitutional (the House of Representatives had overturned the Justice Department's suspension of the alien's deportation). The decision affected clauses in some 200 laws covering a wide range of subjects, including presidential war powers, foreign aid and arms sales, environmental protection, consumer interests, and others. Despite the court's decision, Congress continued to exercise this power, including the legislative veto in at least 11 of the bills it passed in 1984 alone.

Checks and balances that evolved from custom and Constitutional conventions include the congressional committee system and investigative powers, the role of political parties, and presidential influence in initiating legislation.

THE FEDERALIST PAPERS

The proposed Constitution was a well-crafted instrument, but convincing voters that it should be ratified was a project unto itself. Because by late 1787 New York had yet to ratify the Constitution, Alexander Hamilton, James Madison, and John Jay wrote a series of essays on the proposed new Constitution in an effort to persuade New York voters to do so. Formally called *The Federalist*, the Federalist Papers was a series of 85 essays published between 1787 and 1788. Seventy-seven of the essays first appeared serially in New York newspapers, were reprinted in most other states, and were published in book form as *The Federalist* on May 28, 1788; the remaining eight papers appeared in New York newspapers between June 14 and August 16.

The authors of the Federalist Papers presented a masterly defense of the new federal system and of the major departments in the proposed central government. They also argued that the existing government under the Articles of Confederation, the country's first constitution, was defective and that the proposed Constitution would remedy its weaknesses without endangering the liberties of the people.

As a general treatise on republican government, the Federalist Papers are distinguished for their comprehensive analysis of the means by which the ideals of justice, the general welfare, and the rights of individuals could be realized. The authors assumed that the primary political motive of humans was self-interest and that people—whether acting individually or collectively—were selfish and only imperfectly rational. The establishment of a republican form of government would not of itself provide protection against such characteristics: the representatives

For Mrs Church from her sister Elizabeth Hamilton

THE FEDERALIST;

A COLLECTION

OF

E S S A Y S,

WRITTEN IN FAVOUR OF THE

NEW CONSTITUTION,

AS AGREED UPON BY THE FEDERAL CONVENTION,
SEPTEMBER 17, 1787.

IN TWO VOLUMES.

VOL. I.

LIBRARY OF CONGRESS
CITY OF WASHINGTON

NEW-YORK:

PRINTED AND SOLD BY J. AND A. McLEAN,
No. 41, HANOVER-SQUARE.
M,DCC,LXXXVIII.

Mr Jefferson's copy

The Federalist Papers were published in book form as
The Federalist in 1788.

of the people might betray their trust; one segment of the population might oppress another; and both the representatives and the public might give way to passion or caprice. The possibility of good government, they argued, lay in humans' capacity to devise political institutions that would compensate for deficiencies in both reason and virtue in the ordinary conduct of politics. This theme was predominant in late 18th-century political thought in America and accounts in part for the elaborate system of checks and balances that was devised in the Constitution.

In one of the most notable essays, "Federalist 10," Madison rejected the then-common belief that republican government was possible only for small states. He argued that stability, liberty, and justice were more likely to be achieved in a large area with a numerous and heterogeneous population. Although frequently interpreted as an attack on majority rule, the essay is in reality a defense of both social, economic, and cultural pluralism and of a composite majority formed by compromise and conciliation.

"FEDERALIST 10" BY JAMES MADISON

Among the numerous advantages promised by a well-constructed Union, none deserves to be more accurately developed than its tendency to break and control the violence of faction. ... The instability, injustice, and confusion introduced into the public councils have, in truth, been the mortal diseases under which popular governments have everywhere perished. ...

By a faction, I understand a number of citizens, whether amounting to a majority or minority of the whole, who are united and actuated by some common impulse of passion, or of interest, adverse to the rights of other citizens, or to the permanent and aggregate interests of the community. ...

If a faction consists of less than a majority, relief is supplied by the republican principle, which enables the majority to defeat its sinister views by regular vote. ...When a majority is included in a faction, the form of popular government, on the other hand, enables it to sacrifice to its ruling passion or interest both the public good and the rights of other citizens. To secure the public good and private rights against the danger of such a faction, and at the same time to preserve the spirit and the form of popular government, is then the great object to which our inquiries are directed. ...

The two great points of difference between a democracy and a republic are: first, the delegation of the government, in the latter, to a small number of citizens elected by the rest; secondly, the greater number of citizens, and greater sphere of country, over which the latter may be extended.

The effect of the first difference is, on the one hand, to refine and enlarge the public views by

(CONTINUED ON THE NEXT PAGE)

(CONTINUED FROM THE PREVIOUS PAGE)

passing them through the medium of a chosen body of citizens, whose wisdom may best discern the true interest of their country, and whose patriotism and love of justice will be least likely to sacrifice it to temporary or partial considerations. ...

The other point of difference is the greater number of citizens and extent of territory which may be brought within the compass of republican than of democratic government; and it is this circumstance principally which renders factious combinations less to be dreaded in the former than in the latter. The smaller the society, the fewer probably will be the distinct parties and interests composing it; ... and the smaller the number of individuals composing a majority, and the smaller the compass within which they are placed, the more easily will they concert and execute their plans of oppression. Extend the sphere and you ... make it less probable that a majority of the whole will have a common motive to invade the rights of other citizens. ...

In the extent, and proper structure of the Union, therefore, we behold a republican remedy for the diseases most incident to republican government. And according to the degree of pleasure and pride we feel in being republicans, ought to be our zeal in cherishing the spirit and supporting the character of Federalists.

James Madison (1751–1836), fourth president of the United States of America and coauthor of the Federalist Papers.

Decision by such a majority, rather than by a monistic one, would be more likely to accord with the proper ends of government. This distinction between a proper and an improper majority typifies the fundamental philosophy of the Federalist Papers; republican institutions, including the principle of majority rule, were not considered good in themselves but were good because they constituted the best means for the pursuit of justice and the preservation of liberty.

All the papers appeared over the signature "Publius," and the authorship of some of the papers was once a matter of scholarly dispute. However, computer analysis and historical evidence has led nearly all historians to assign authorship in the following manner: Hamilton wrote numbers 1, 6–9, 11–13, 15–17, 21–36, 59–61, and 65–85; Madison, numbers 10, 14, 18–20, 37–58, and 62–63; and Jay, numbers 2–5 and 64.

CONSTITUTIONAL ADJUDICATION

In a few U.S. states and in many countries, questions as to the constitutional validity of a statute may be referred in abstract form to a high court by the chief executive or the legislature for an advisory opinion. In most systems, however, this is unusual and, in any event, supplementary to the normal procedure of raising and deciding constitutional questions. The normal pattern is for a constitutional question to be raised at the trial-court level in the context of a genuine controversy and decided finally on appellate review of the trial-court decision.

The U.S. pattern of constitutional adjudication is not followed in all countries that have written constitutions. In some countries (e.g., Germany), there is a special court at the highest level of government that handles only constitutional questions and to which all such questions are referred as soon as they arise and before any concrete controversy occurs. A constitutional question may be referred to the special court in abstract form for a declaratory opinion by a procedure similar to that prevailing in the minority of U.S. states that allow advisory opinions. In France, members of the parliament may demand (and increasingly have demanded) that the constitutionality of legislation be certified by the Constitutional Council prior to its becoming law.

In other countries, written constitutions may be in effect but not accompanied by any conception that their authoritative interpretation is a judicial function. Legislative and executive bodies, rather than courts, act as the guardians and interpreters of the constitution, being guided by their provisions but not bound by them in any realistic sense. Modernization in the developing world, the spread of democracy in Latin America in the 1980s and '90s, and the collapse of communism in the states of the former Soviet Union and eastern Europe in 1989–91 have meant that there are now fewer instances of wholly impotent courts. Still, in some countries, the courts remain captive to political elites or open to manipulation by the government, or the courts' authority to exercise the judicial review to which they are constitutionally entitled remains tenuous. In 1993, for example, the Russian constitutional court was dissolved by President Boris Yeltsin and replaced with a system of appointments that ensured greater presidential control.

Finally, some countries, such as the United Kingdom, have no formal written constitution. In such countries, parliamentary supremacy clearly prevails, though European law (i.e., the law of the European Union [EU]) now supersedes parliamentary supremacy in all EU countries. In the United Kingdom, Brexit (as the UK's controversial vote on June 23, 2016 to withdraw from the EU has come to be known) will obviously mark a change in this policy. The courts have only limited power to invalidate statutes, though they can and do interpret them, which is a very important judicial power.

CHAPTER FIVE

FEDERAL VERSUS STATE POWER

Many political battles in U.S. history have been based on conflicting interpretations of the extent of the implied powers granted to the federal government by the U.S. Constitution. Historically, proponents of the rights of states, or states' rights, particularly in the South, upheld a narrow interpretation of the implied powers of the federal government and an expansive interpretation of the residual powers of the state governments. An extreme example of this view was the historical doctrine of nullification, according to which states have the power to nullify within their boundaries any act of the federal government with which they disagree.

STATES' RIGHTS

States' rights are the rights or powers retained by the state, provincial, or regional governments of a federal union under the provisions of a federal constitution. In the United States, Switzerland, and Australia, the powers of the regional governments are those that remain after the powers of the central government have been enumerated in the constitution. In contrast, the powers at both the state or regional level and the national level of government are defined clearly by specific provisions of the constitutions of Canada and Germany.

The concept of states' rights is closely related to that of state rights, which was invoked from the 18th century in Europe to legitimate the powers vested in sovereign national governments. Doctrines asserting states' rights were developed in contexts in which states functioned as distinct units in a federal system of government. In the United States, for example, Americans in the 18th and 19th centuries often referred to the rights of states, implying that each state had inherent rights and sovereignty. Before and following the American Civil War (1861–65), the U.S. states—particularly the Southern states—shared the belief that each of them was sovereign and should have jurisdiction over its most important affairs. Today the term is applied more broadly to a variety of efforts aimed at reducing the powers of national governments, which had grown considerably in both size and scope.

Advocates of states' rights put greater trust and confidence in regional or state governments than in national ones. State governments, according to them, are more responsive to popular control, more sensitive to state issues and problems, and more understanding of the culture and values of the state's population than are national governments. For these reasons, they argue, state governments are better able to address important problems and protect individual rights. In the United States, states' rights proponents also have maintained that strong state governments are more consistent with the vision of republican government put forward by the Founding Fathers. They cite in support of their view the Tenth Amendment to the U.S. Constitution, which reserves for the states the residue of powers "not delegated to the United States by the Constitution, nor prohibited by it to the States."

In the United States, the term "states' rights" has been applied to a variety of political programs. Before the American Civil War, it was the rallying cry of Southern

The Texas State Capitol building is in Austin. State legislatures pass many of the laws that govern citizens' lives.

opponents of Northern-inspired tariffs and Northern proposals to abolish or restrict slavery. The notion of states' rights also was used as an argument for the doctrine of nullification and for the claim that the states, by virtue of their sovereignty, had the right to secede from the Union. This constitutional question was resolved only by the victory of the North (federal government) in the Civil War. A century later the doctrine was used to justify opposition to the federal government's efforts to enforce racial desegregation.

Such uses of the doctrine of states' rights in the United States and elsewhere prompted some critics to claim that it serves parochial interests. According to them, states' rights are invoked by majorities in the states to justify laws and practices that discriminate against various ethnic, religious, or other minority groups. They contend that a strong national government is necessary to ensure that states respect the rights guaranteed to all citizens in the national constitution.

States' rights advocates also addressed issues related to environmental protection and education. In the western United States, for example, some citizen groups questioned the power of the federal government to issue pollution standards and regulations on water and land use, arguing that they amounted to an unconstitutional infringement on the right of states to manage their own natural resources. Many states also resisted the imposition of national educational testing standards out of concern that they would undermine the states' historical control over education.

NULLIFICATION

Nullification is the doctrine in U.S. history that upheld the right of a state to declare null and void within its boundaries an act of the federal government. Thomas Jefferson and James Madison advocated nullification in the Virginia and Kentucky Resolutions of 1798. The Union was a compact of sovereign states, Jefferson asserted, and the federal government was their agent with certain specified, delegated powers. The states retained the authority to determine when the federal government exceeded its powers, and they could declare acts to be "void and of no force" in their jurisdictions.

John C. Calhoun furthered the nullification doctrine in his *South Carolina Exposition and Protest*, published and distributed by the South Carolina legislature (without Calhoun's name on it) in 1829. Writing in response to Southern bitterness over the Tariff of 1828 ("Tariff of Abominations"), Calhoun took the position that state "interposition" could block enforcement of a federal law. The state would be obliged to obey only if the law were made an amendment to the Constitution by three-fourths of the states. The "concurrent majority"—i.e., the people of a state having veto power over federal actions—would protect minority rights from the possible tyranny of the numerical majority.

When the Tariff of 1832 only slightly modified the Tariff of 1828, the South Carolina legislature decided to put Calhoun's nullification theory to a practical test. The legislature called for a special state convention, and on November 24, 1832, the convention adopted the Ordinance of Nullification. The ordinance declared the tariffs of 1828 and 1832 "null, void, and no law, nor binding upon this State, its officers or citizens." It also forbade appeal of any ordinance measure to the federal courts, required all state officeholders (except members of the legislature) to take an oath of support for the ordinance, and threatened secession if the federal government tried to collect tariff duties by force. In its attempts to have other Southern states join in nullification, however, South Carolina met with total failure.

On December 10, 1832, President Andrew Jackson issued his "Proclamation to the People of South Carolina," asserting the supremacy of the federal government and warning that "disunion by armed force is treason." Congress then (March 1, 1833) passed both the Force Bill—authorizing Jackson to use the military if necessary to collect tariff duties—and a compromise tariff that reduced those duties. The South Carolina convention responded on March 15 by rescinding the Ordinance of Nullification but three days later maintained its principles by nullifying the Force Bill.

As a consequence of the nullification crisis, Jackson emerged a hero to nationalists. But Southerners were

Andrew Jackson, American soldier and statesman, served as the seventh president of the United States (1829–37).

made more conscious of their minority position and more aware of their vulnerability to a Northern majority as long as they remained in the Union.

FEDERAL SYSTEMS OF GOVERNMENT

The U.S. Constitution embodies a mode of political organization known as federalism. Federal systems of government unite separate states or other polities within an overarching political system in such a way as to allow each to maintain its own fundamental political integrity. Federal systems do this by requiring that basic policies be made and implemented through negotiation in some form, so that all the members can share in making and executing decisions. The political principles that animate federal systems emphasize the primacy of bargaining and negotiated coordination among several power centres; they stress the virtues of dispersed power centres (separation of powers) as a means for safeguarding individual and local liberties.

The various political systems that call themselves federal differ in many ways. Certain characteristics and principles, however, are common to all truly federal systems: a written constitution, noncentralization of power, and areal (or geographic) division of power.

ELEMENTS MAINTAINING UNION

Modern federal systems generally provide direct lines of communication between the citizenry and all the governments that serve them. The people may and usually

PRINCIPLES OF FEDERAL SYSTEMS

WRITTEN CONSTITUTION:

First, the federal relationship must be established or confirmed through a perpetual covenant of union, usually embodied in a written constitution that outlines the terms by which power is divided or shared; the constitution can be altered only by extraordinary procedures. These constitutions are distinctive in being not simply compacts between rulers and ruled but involving the people, the general government, and the states constituting the federal union. The constituent states, moreover, often retain constitution-making rights of their own.

NONCENTRALIZATION:

Second, the political system itself must reflect the constitution by actually diffusing power among a number of substantially self-sustaining centers. Such a diffusion of power may be termed non-centralization. Noncentralization is a way of ensuring in practice that the authority to participate in exercising political power cannot be taken away from the general or the state governments without common consent.

(CONTINUED ON THE NEXT PAGE)

(CONTINUED FROM THE PREVIOUS PAGE)

A REAL DIVISION OF POWER:

A third element of any federal system is what has been called in the United States territorial democracy. This has two faces: the use of areal (geographic) divisions to ensure neutrality and equality in the representation of the various groups and interests in the polity and the use of such divisions to secure local autonomy and representation for diverse groups within the same civil society. Territorial neutrality has proved highly useful in societies that are changing, allowing for the representation of new interests in proportion to their strength simply by allowing their supporters to vote in relatively equal territorial units. At the same time, the accommodation of very diverse groups whose differences are fundamental rather than transient by giving them

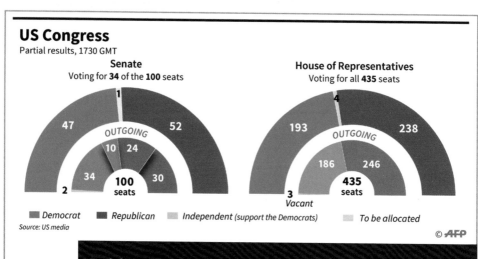

US Congress
Partial results, 1730 GMT

Senate
Voting for **34** of the **100** seats

47 — OUTGOING — 52
1
10   24
34   100 seats   30
2

House of Representatives
Voting for all **435** seats

193 — OUTGOING — 238
4
186   246
435 seats
3 Vacant

Democrat   Republican   Independent (support the Democrats)   To be allocated

Source: US media

© AFP

Both houses of the U.S. Congress usually have many members of both parties, but in some states most representatives are from the same party, such as Democrats in California and Republicans in Texas. Other states, such as Illinois and Florida, are more evenly split between the parties.

territorial power bases of their own has enhanced the ability of federal systems to function as vehicles of political integration while preserving democratic government. One example of this system may be seen in Canada, which includes a population of French descent, centred in the province of Quebec.

do elect representatives to all the governments, and all of them may and usually do administer programs that directly serve the individual citizen.

The existence of those direct lines of communication is one of the features distinguishing federations from leagues or confederations. It is usually based on a sense of common nationality binding the constituent polities and people together. In some countries, this sense of nationality has been inherited, as in Germany, while in the United States, Argentina, and Australia it had to be at least partly invented. Canada and Switzerland have had to evolve this sense in order to hold together strongly divergent nationality groups. In the relatively new federal systems of India, Malaysia, and Nigeria, the future of federalism is endangered by the absence of such a common national sense.

Geographic necessity has played a part in promoting the maintenance of union within federal systems. The Mississippi Valley in the United States, the Alps in Switzerland, the island character of the Australian continent, and the mountains and jungles surrounding Brazil have all

In Louisiana, a barge travels down the Mississippi River, a major geographic feature of the United States.

been influences promoting unity; so have the pressures for Canadian union arising from that country's situation on the border of the United States and the pressures upon the German states generated by their neighbors to the east and west. In this connection, the necessity for a common defense against common enemies has stimulated federal union in the first place and acted to maintain it.

ELEMENTS MAINTAINING THE FEDERAL PRINCIPLE

Several devices found in federal systems serve to maintain the federal principle itself. Two of these are of particular importance.

The maintenance of federalism requires that the nation and its constituent polities each have substantially complete governing institutions of their own, with the right to modify those institutions unilaterally within limits set by the compact. Both separate legislative and separate administrative institutions are necessary.

The contractual sharing of public responsibilities by all governments in the system appears to be a central characteristic of federalism. Sharing, broadly conceived, includes common involvement in policy making, financing, and administration. Sharing may be formal or informal; in federal systems, it is usually contractual. The contract is used as a legal device to enable governments to engage in joint action while remaining independent entities. Even where there is no formal arrangement, the spirit of federalism tends to infuse a sense of contractual obligation.

Federal systems or systems strongly influenced by federal principles have been among the most stable and long-lasting of polities. But the successful operation of federal systems requires a particular kind of political environment, one that is conducive to popular government and has the requisite traditions of political cooperation and self-restraint. Beyond this, federal systems operate best in societies with sufficient homogeneity of fundamental interests to allow a great deal of latitude to local government and to permit reliance upon voluntary collaboration. The use of force to maintain domestic order is even more inimical to the successful maintenance of federal patterns of government than to other forms of popular government. Federal systems are most successful in societies that have the human resources to fill many public offices competently and the material resources to afford a measure of economic waste as part of the price of liberty.

CHAPTER SIX

Due Process in Constitutional History

Due process is a course of legal proceedings according to rules and principles that have been established in a system of jurisprudence for the enforcement and protection of private rights. Through one of its more controversial interpretations, the U.S. Supreme Court found (*Roe* v. *Wade*, 1973; *Planned Parenthood of Southeastern Pennsylvania* v. *Casey*, 1992 ; *Whole Woman's Health* v. *Hellerstedt*, 2016) that a woman's constitutional right to privacy entitles her to obtain an abortion freely, prior to the point at which the fetus attains viability.

In each case, due process contemplates an exercise of the powers of government as the law permits and sanctions, under recognized safeguards for the protection of individual rights. Principally associated with one of the fundamental guarantees of the United States Constitution, due process derives from early English common law and constitutional history.

THE MEANING OF DUE PROCESS

The first concrete expression of the idea of due process embraced by Anglo-American law appeared in the 39th article of Magna Carta (1215) in the royal promise that "No freeman shall be taken or (and) imprisoned or disseised or exiled or in any way destroyed . . . except by the legal judgment of his peers or (and) by the law of the land." In subsequent English statutes, the references to "the legal judgment of his peers" and "laws of the land" are treated as substantially synonymous with due process of law. Drafters of the U.S. federal Constitution adopted the due-process phraseology in the Fifth Amendment, ratified in 1791, which provides that "No person shall . . . be deprived of life, liberty, or property, without due process of law." Because this amendment was held inapplicable to state

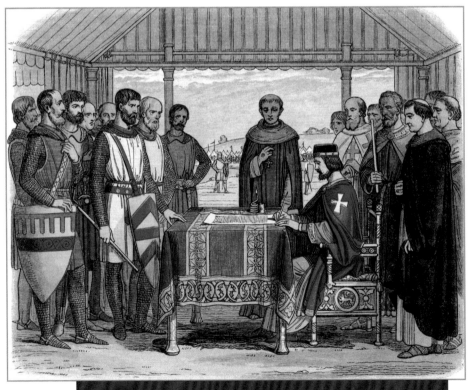

King John signs the Magna Carta on June 15, 1215, at Runnymede, England.

actions that might violate an individual's constitutional rights, it was not until the ratification of the Fourteenth Amendment in 1868 that the several states became subject to a federally enforceable due-process restraint on their legislative and procedural activities.

The meaning of due process as it relates to substantive enactments and procedural legislation has evolved over decades of controversial interpretation by the Supreme Court. Today, if a law may reasonably be deemed to promote the public welfare and the means selected bear a reasonable relationship to the legitimate public interest, then the law has met the due-process standard. If the law seeks to regulate a fundamental right, such as the right to travel or the right to vote, then this enactment must meet a stricter judicial scrutiny, known as the compelling interest test. Economic legislation is generally upheld if the state can point to any conceivable public benefit resulting from its enactment.

In determining the procedural safeguards that should be obligatory upon the states under the due-process clause of the Fourteenth Amendment, the Supreme Court has exercised considerable supervision over the administration of criminal justice in state courts, as well as occasional influence upon state civil and administrative proceedings. Its decisions have been vigorously criticized, on the one hand, for unduly meddling with state judicial administration and, on the other hand, for not treating all of the specific procedural guarantees of the first 10 amendments as equally applicable to state and to federal proceedings.

THE FIFTH AMENDMENT

No person shall be held to answer for a capital, or otherwise infamous crime, unless on a presentment or indictment of a Grand Jury, except in cases arising in the land or naval forces, or in the Militia, when in actual service in time of War or public danger; nor shall any person be subject for the same offence to be twice put in jeopardy of life or limb; nor shall be compelled in any criminal case to be a witness against himself, nor be deprived of life, liberty, or property, without due process of law; nor shall private property be taken for public use without just compensation.

Some justices have adhered to the proposition that the framers of the Fourteenth Amendment intended the entire Bill of Rights to be binding on the states. They have asserted that this position would provide an objective basis for reviewing state activities and would promote a desirable uniformity between state and federal rights and sanctions. Other justices, however, have contended that states should be allowed considerable latitude in conducting their affairs, so long as they comply with a fundamental fairness standard. Ultimately, the latter position substantially prevailed, and due process was recognized as embracing only those principles of justice that are "so rooted in the traditions and conscience of our people as to be ranked as fundamental." In fact, however, almost all of the Bill of Rights has by now been included among those fundamental principles.

The due-process clause has been interpreted and applied by the U.S. Supreme Court in a number of landmark cases. Two of the most significant of these decisions were the Slaughterhouse Cases (1873) and *Adair* v. *United States* (1908).

THE SLAUGHTERHOUSE CASES

The Slaughterhouse Cases were a set of legal cases that resulted in 1873 in a landmark U.S. Supreme Court decision limiting the protection of the privileges and immunities clause of the Fourteenth Amendment to the U.S. Constitution.

In 1869 the Louisiana state legislature granted a monopoly of the New Orleans slaughtering business to a single corporation. Other slaughterhouses brought suit, contending that the monopoly abridged their privileges and immunities as U.S. citizens and deprived them of property without due process of law. When the suit reached the Supreme Court in 1873, it presented the first test of the Fourteenth Amendment, ratified in 1868.

By a 5–4 majority, the Court ruled against the other slaughterhouses. Associate Justice Samuel F. Miller, for the

EQUAL PROTECTION AND THE CIVIL RIGHTS ACT

In 1995 and 1997, respectively, Jennifer Gratz and Patrick Hamacher, both of whom were white, were denied admission to the University of Michigan's School of Literature, Science, and the Arts (LSA). The two filed a class-action suit alleging racial discrimination in violation of the equal-protection clause and Title VI of the Civil Rights Act (1964), which assures nondiscrimination in the distribution of funds under federally assisted programs. The admissions policy then used by the LSA, which was aimed at achieving racial diversity within the student body, automatically awarded points to candidates whose race was African American, Hispanic, or Native American. The court ruled by a 6–3 majority that the LSA's use of race or ethnicity in its admissions policy too closely approximated the racial quotas that the court had determined were inconsistent with the equal-protection clause in *Regents of the University of California* v. *Bakke* (1978). The court's opinion was written by Chief Justice William Rehnquist.

In 1997 Barbara Grutter, who was white, was denied admission to the University of Michigan Law School despite being well-qualified academically; she filed suit alleging violation of the equal-protection clause and Title VI. The admissions policy used by the school took the race of the candidate into account without granting an automatic and significant advantage to certain candidates on the basis of race or ethnicity. However, in *Grutter* v. *Bollinger*, the court ruled by a 5–4 majority that the school's admissions policy did *not* violate the equal-protection clause or Title VI because it used race in a "narrowly tailored" and "holistic" manner within a system of highly individualized interviews, treating race or ethnicity as merely a "'plus' in a particular applicant's file," as recommended by Justice Lewis F. Powell in his concurring opinion in *Bakke*. The court's opinion in *Gratz* was written by Justice Sandra Day O'Connor.

majority, declared that the Fourteenth Amendment had "one pervading purpose": protection of the newly emancipated African Americans. The amendment did not, however, shift control over all civil rights from the states to the federal government. States still retained legal jurisdiction over their citizens, and federal protection of civil rights did not extend to the property rights of businessmen.

Dissenting justices held that the Fourteenth Amendment protected all U.S. citizens from state violations of privileges and immunities and that state impairment of property rights was a violation of due process.

The Slaughterhouse Cases represented a temporary reversal in the trend toward centralization of power in the federal government. More importantly, in limiting the protection of the privileges and immunities clause, the court unwittingly weakened the power of the Fourteenth Amendment to protect the civil rights of African Americans.

ADAIR V. UNITED STATES

In its *Adair* v. *United States* ruling, issued on January 27, 1908, the U.S. Supreme Court upheld so-called "yellow dog" contracts forbidding workers from joining labour unions. William Adair of the Louisville and Nashville Railroad fired O.B. Coppage for belonging to a labour

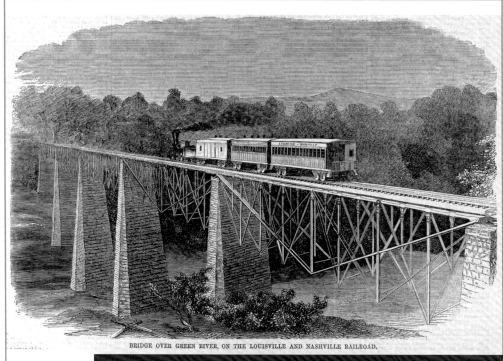

BRIDGE OVER GREEN RIVER, ON THE LOUISVILLE AND NASHVILLE RAILROAD.

The Louisville and Nashville Railroad crosses the Green River. The railroad company was found in direct violation of the Erdman Act of 1898 after William Adair fired O.B. Coppage, for belonging to a labor union.

union, an action in direct violation of the Erdman Act of 1898, which prohibited railroads engaged in interstate commerce from requiring workers to refrain from union membership as a condition of employment. In 1908 the Supreme Court decided in a 6–2 vote that the Erdman Act was unconstitutional. The court held that the act represented an unreasonable violation of the due process clause of the Fifth Amendment, which guaranteed freedom of contract and property rights; moreover, according to the majority, Congress's constitutional authority over interstate commerce did not extend to matters of union membership.

CHAPTER SEVEN

PROTECTIONS OF THE FIRST AMENDMENT

Freedom of religion is defined as the right to practice one's own religion. Freedom of speech refers to the right to express information, ideas, and opinions free of government restrictions based on content. It encompasses freedom of the press, which is the right of individuals, companies, or other organizations to publish, broadcast, or otherwise disseminate information without prior (prepublication) restraint or censorship or post-publication sanction by the government. In the United States the freedoms of speech and of the press are guaranteed by the First Amendment to the Constitution:

Congress shall make no law respecting an establishment of religion, or prohibiting the free exercise thereof; or abridging the freedom of speech, or of the press; or the right of the people peaceably to assemble, and to petition the Government for a redress of grievances.

These freedoms are not absolute. Since the early 20th century, the Supreme Court has permitted restrictions on speech and the press in cases in which there is a risk or threat to safety or other public interests that is serious and imminent.

The inherent ambiguity of constitutional interpretation can be seen clearly by considering the First Amendment to the Constitution of the United States, which states that "Congress shall make no law . . . abridging the freedom of speech." This prescription, upon first glance, seems entirely clear. Nevertheless, few people—not least the framers of the Constitution—have interpreted it as meaning that Congress cannot pass any law that abridges any form of speech. Most would also accept at least some legal restrictions on libelous speech, and many would accept restrictions on hate speech. Indeed, once one begins to consider the wide variety of actions that might qualify as speech (including "nonverbal," or symbolic, speech), it is easy to conclude that the U.S. Constitution itself has little literal meaning beyond what is given to it by the interpretations of judges.

SEPARATION OF CHURCH AND STATE

Church and state is the belief, largely Christian in origin, that the religious and political powers in society are or should be clearly distinct, though both claim the people's loyalty.

Before the advent of Christianity, separate religious and political orders were not clearly defined in most civilizations. People worshipped the gods of the particular state in which they lived, religion in such cases being but a department of the state. In the case of the Jewish people, the revealed Law of the Scripture constituted the Law of Israel. The Christian concept of the secular and the spiritual is founded on the words of Jesus: "Render to Caesar the things that are Caesar's, and to God the things that are God's" (Mark 12:17). Two distinct, but not altogether separate, areas of human life and activity had to be distinguished; hence, a theory of two powers came to form the basis of Christian thought and teaching from earliest times.

By the 17th century, however, there were few who believed that diversity of religious belief and a church unconnected with the civil power were possible in a unified state. Common religious standards were looked upon as a principal support of the political order. When the notions of diversity of belief and toleration of dissent did start to grow, they were not generally seen to conflict with the concept of a state church. The Puritans, for example, who fled religious persecution in England in the 17th century, enforced rigid conformity to church ideas among settlers in the American colonies.

The concept of secular government as expressed in the First Amendment to the U.S. Constitution reflected both the influence of the French Enlightenment on colonial intellectuals and the special interests of the established churches in preserving their separate and distinct identities. The Baptists, notably, held the separation of church and state powers as a principle of their creed.

The great wave of migration to the United States by Roman Catholics in the 1840s prompted a reassertion of the principle of secular government by state legislatures fearing allocation of government funds to parochial educational facilities. The 20th century saw the First and Fourteenth amendments to the Constitution applied with considerable strictness by the courts in the field of education. Late in the century, conservative Christian groups in the United States generated considerable controversy by seeking textbook censorship, reversal of court prohibition of school prayer, and requirements that certain Biblical doctrines be taught alongside scientific theories, in particular the theory of human evolution.

ENGEL V. VITALE

In *Engel* v. *Vitale*, on June 25, 1962, the U.S. Supreme Court ruled that voluntary prayer in public schools violated the U.S. Constitution's First Amendment.

The west facade of the U.S. Supreme Court building.

New York state's Board of Regents wrote and authorized a voluntary nondenominational prayer that could be recited by students at the beginning of each school day. In 1958–59 a group of parents that included Steven Engel in Hyde Park, New York, objected to the prayer, which read, "Almighty God, we acknowledge our dependence upon Thee, and beg Thy blessings upon us, our teachers, and our country," and sued the school board president, William Vitale. The prayer, which proponents argued was constitutional because it was voluntary and promoted the free exercise of religion (also protected in the First Amendment), was upheld by New York's courts, prompting the petitioners to file a successful appeal to the U.S. Supreme Court.

Oral arguments took place on April 3, 1962. The Supreme Court's ruling was released on June 25 and found New York's law unconstitutional by a margin of 6–1 (two justices did not participate in the decision). Hugo L. Black wrote the Supreme Court's opinion, in which the majority argued "that, by using its public school system to encourage recitation of the Regents' prayer, the State of New York has adopted a practice wholly inconsistent with the Establishment Clause." The lone dissent came from Potter Stewart, who argued that the majority had "misapplied a great constitutional principle" and could not understand "how an 'official religion' is established by letting those who want to say a prayer say it. On the contrary, I think to deny the wish of these school children to join in reciting this prayer is to deny them the opportunity of

WEST VIRGINIA STATE BOARD OF EDUCATION V. BARNETTE

In *West Virginia State Board of Education* v. *Barnette*, decided on June 14, 1943, the U.S. Supreme Court ruled that compelling children in public schools to salute the U.S. flag was an unconstitutional violation of their freedom of speech and religion.

On the heels of *Minersville School District (Pennsylvania)* v. *Gobitis* (1940), in which the Supreme Court upheld (8–1) the school district's expulsion of two students for refusing to salute the flag on the basis of religious grounds (the children were Jehovah's Witnesses), West Virginia enacted a rule in 1942 that required students to salute the U.S. flag. Walter Barnette, a Jehovah's Witness in West Virginia, sued in U.S. district court and won an injunction against state enforcement of the rule. The state school board appealed to the U.S. Supreme Court, which agreed to hear the case.

Oral arguments were held on March 11, 1943, and the ruling was issued on June 14. In a 6–3 decision the court overturned the *Gobitis* ruling. The majority opinion was written by Justice Robert H. Jackson, who had voted with the majority in *Gobitis*. While the earlier decision had focused primarily on claims of freedom

(CONTINUED ON THE NEXT PAGE)

(CONTINUED FROM THE PREVIOUS PAGE)

of religion protections in the U.S. Constitution's First Amendment, the *Barnette* ruling invoked both freedom of religion and an individual's freedom of speech—and that freedom of speech included the right not to be forced to speak against one's will. Jackson's opinion underscored the rights of minorities against the tyranny of the majority: "If there is any fixed star in our constitutional constellation, it is that no official, high or petty, can prescribe what shall be orthodox in politics, nationalism, religion, or other matters of opinion, or force citizens to confess by word or act their faith therein." And, attempting to capture the essence of the Bill of Rights protections, Jackson wrote: "The very purpose of a Bill of Rights was to withdraw certain subjects from the vicissitudes of political controversy, to place them beyond the reach of majorities and officials and to establish them as legal principles to be applied by the courts. One's right to life, liberty, and property, to free speech, a free press, freedom of worship and assembly, and other fundamental rights may not be submitted to vote; they depend on the outcome of no elections."

sharing in the spiritual heritage of our Nation." The decision, the first in which the Supreme Court had ruled unconstitutional public school sponsorship of religion, was unpopular with a broad segment of the American public.

SCHENCK V. UNITED STATES

Schenck v. *United States* was a legal case in which, on March 3, 1919, the U.S. Supreme Court ruled that the freedom of speech protection afforded in the U.S. Constitution's First Amendment could be restricted if the words spoken or printed represented to society a "clear and present danger."

In June 1917, shortly after U.S. entry into World War I, Congress passed the Espionage Act, which made it illegal during wartime to:

> *willfully make or convey false reports or false statements with intent to interfere with the operation or success of the military or naval forces of the United States or to promote the success of its enemies . . . [or] willfully cause or attempt to cause insubordination, disloyalty, mutiny, or refusal of duty, in the military or naval forces of the United States, or shall willfully obstruct the recruiting or enlistment service of the United States, to the injury of the service or of the United States.*

Charles T. Schenck was general secretary of the U.S. Socialist Party, which opposed the implementation of a military draft in the country. The party printed and distributed some 15,000 leaflets that called for men who were drafted to resist military service. Schenck was subsequently arrested for having violated the Espionage Act; he was convicted on three counts and sentenced to 10 years in prison for each count.

Judge Jacob Panken, a member of the Socialist Party, speaks at an anti-war rally in Union Square, 1914.

Oral arguments at the Supreme Court were heard on January 9, 1919, with Schenck's counsel arguing that the Espionage Act was unconstitutional and that his client was simply exercising his freedom of speech guaranteed by the First Amendment. On March 3 the court issued a unanimous ruling upholding the Espionage Act and Schenck's conviction. Writing for the court, Justice Oliver Wendell Holmes, Jr., argued:

The character of every act depends upon the circumstances in which it is done. The most stringent protection of free speech would not protect a man in falsely shouting fire in a theatre and causing a panic. [The] question in every case is whether the words used are used in such circumstances and are of such a nature as to create a clear and present danger that they will bring about the substantive evils that Congress has a right to prevent.

Throughout the 1920s, however, the court abandoned the clear and present danger rule and instead utilized an earlier-devised "bad [or dangerous] tendency" doctrine, which enabled speech to be limited even more broadly.

GITLOW V. NEW YORK

The Supreme Court's *Gitlow* v. *New York* ruling of June 8, 1925, held that the U.S. Constitution's First Amendment protection of free speech, which states that the federal "Congress shall make no law . . . abridging the freedom of speech," applied also to state governments. The decision was the first in which the Supreme Court held that the Fourteenth Amendment's due-process clause required state and federal governments to be held to the same standards in regulating speech.

The case arose in November 1919 when Benjamin Gitlow, who had served as a local assemblyman, and an associate, Alan Larkin, were arrested by New York City police officers for criminal anarchy, an offense under New York state law. Gitlow and Larkin were both Communist Party members and publishers of the *Revolutionary Age*, a

The U.S. government's Subversive Activities Control Board (SACB) opens public hearings on the registration of the Communist Party with Benjamin Gitlow (*lower left*) as the first witness, in Washington, April 23, 1951.

radical newspaper in which they printed "The Left Wing Manifesto" (modeled on *The Communist Manifesto* by Karl Marx and Friedrich Engels), which advocated the violent overthrow of the U.S. government. Although Gitlow argued at trial that no violent action was precipitated by the article, he was convicted, and the conviction was subsequently upheld by the state appellate court.

Oral arguments before the Supreme Court took place in April and November 1923, and the Supreme Court issued its ruling, written by Justice Edward T. Sanford, in June 1925. The court upheld Gitlow's conviction, but perhaps ironically the ruling expanded free speech protections for individuals, since the court held that the First Amendment was applicable to state governments through the due-process clause of the Fourteenth Amendment. The majority opinion stipulated that the court "assume[s] that freedom of speech and of the press which are protected by the First Amendment from abridgment by Congress are among the fundamental personal rights and 'liberties' protected by the due process clause of the Fourteenth Amendment from impairment by the States." In ruling that the conviction was constitutional, however, the court rejected the "clear and present danger" test established in *Schenck* v. *United States* (1919) and instead used the "bad (or dangerous) tendency" test. The New York state law was constitutional because the state "cannot reasonably be required to defer the adoption of measures for its own peace and safety until the revolutionary utterances lead to actual disturbances of the public peace or imminent and immediate danger of its own destruction; but it may, in the exercise of its judgment, suppress the threatened danger in its incipiency." In an eloquent dissenting opinion, Justices Oliver Wendell Holmes, Jr., and Louis Brandeis held to the clear and present danger test, arguing that:

there was no present danger of an attempt to overthrow the government by force on the part of the admittedly small minority who shared the defendant's views . . . . If the publication of this document had been laid as an attempt to induce an uprising against government at once and not at some indefinite time in the future it would have presented a different question . . . . But the indictment alleges the publication and nothing more.

The ruling, which enabled prohibitions on speech that simply advocated potential violence, was eventually dismissed by the Supreme Court in the 1930s and later as the court became more restrictive in the types of speech that government could permissibly suppress.

DENNIS V. UNITED STATES

On June 4, 1951, in *Dennis* v. *United States*, the U.S. Supreme Court upheld the constitutionality of the Smith Act (1940), which made it a criminal offense to advocate the violent overthrow of the government or to organize or be a member of any group or society devoted to such advocacy.

The case originated in 1948 when Eugene Dennis, general secretary of the American Communist Party, along with several other high-ranking communists, was arrested and convicted of having violated the Smith Act. The conviction was upheld by lower courts, despite the fact that no evidence existed that Dennis and his colleagues had encouraged any of their followers to commit specific violent acts, and was appealed to the Supreme Court, which agreed to hear the case.

Leaders of the American Communist Party leave court in handcuffs after being found guilty of conspiring to teach the overthrow of the United States government by violence.

Against the backdrop of the case was a growing fear in the United States during the Cold War of a communist takeover of the country. Oral arguments were held on December 1, 1950, and on the following June 4 the Supreme Court issued a 6–2 ruling upholding the convictions, in essence finding that it was constitutional to restrict the guarantee of freedom of speech found in the U.S. Constitution's First Amendment when an individual's speech was so grave that it represented a vital threat to the security of the country. The court's plurality opinion was written by Chief Justice Fred M. Vinson, joined by Justices Harold Burton, Sherman Minton, and Stanley

Reed, who argued: "Certainly an attempt to overthrow the Government by force, even though doomed from the outset because of inadequate numbers or power of the revolutionists, is a sufficient evil for Congress to prevent." The ruling further maintained that government need not wait to prohibit speech "until the putsch is about to be executed, the plans have been laid and the signal is awaited. If Government is aware that a group aiming at its overthrow is attempting to indoctrinate its members and to commit them to a course whereby they will strike when the leaders feel the circumstances permit, action by the Government is required." Two other justices, Felix Frankfurter and Robert H. Jackson, voted with the majority but wrote special concurrences that deviated somewhat from the ruling's overall logic. Frankfurter, in particular, argued that Congress needed to balance free speech protections against the threat of that speech. The court's opinion ran somewhat contrary to the clear and present danger rule of Justice Oliver Wendell Holmes, Jr., in *Schenck* v. *United States* in 1919, which required that immediate violence or danger be present for speech to be lawfully limited.

Dissenting from the majority were Justices Hugo L. Black, who had developed a literal interpretation of the Bill of Rights and an absolutist position on First Amendment rights, and William O. Douglas. Black's eloquent opinion both captured the tenor of the times and was a strong defense of freedom of speech:

So long as this Court exercises the power of judicial review of legislation, I cannot agree that the First Amendment permits U.S. to sustain laws suppressing freedom of speech and press on the basis of Congress' or our own notions of mere 'reasonableness.' . . . . Public opinion being what it now is, few will protest the conviction of these Communist petitioners. There is hope, however, that, in calmer times, when present pressures, passions and fears subside, this or some later Court will restore the First Amendment liberties to the high preferred place where they belong in a free society.

In *Yates* v. *United States* (1957), the court later amended its ruling to make parts of the Smith Act unenforceable, and though the law remained on the books, no prosecutions took place under it thereafter.

THE PENTAGON PAPERS AND THE *PROGRESSIVE*

One of the most dramatic 20th-century attempts by the government of the United States to exercise prior restraint occurred in connection with the Pentagon Papers, a top secret multivolume history of the U.S. role in Indochina from World War II until May 1968 that was commissioned in 1967 by U.S. Secretary of Defense Robert S. McNamara. The papers were turned over (without authorization) to the *New York Times* by Daniel Ellsberg, a senior research associate at the

Massachusetts Institute of Technology's Center for International Studies.

The 47-volume history, consisting of approximately 3,000 pages of narrative and 4,000 pages of appended documents, took 18 months to complete. Ellsberg, who worked on the project, had been an ardent early supporter of the U.S. role in Indochina but, by the project's end, had become seriously opposed to U.S. involvement. He felt compelled to reveal the nature of U.S. participation and leaked major portions of the papers to the press.

On June 13, 1971, the *New York Times* began publishing a series of articles based on the study. After the third daily installment appeared in the *Times*, the U.S. Department of Justice obtained in U.S. District Court a temporary restraining order against further publication of the classified material, contending that further public dissemination of the material would cause "immediate and irreparable harm" to U.S. national-defense interests.

The *Times*—joined by the *Washington Post*, which also was in possession of the documents—fought the order through the courts for the next 15 days, during which time publication of the series was suspended. On June 30, 1971, the U.S. Supreme Court, in a 6–3 decision, freed the newspapers to resume publishing the material. The court held that the government had failed to justify restraint of publication.

The Pentagon Papers revealed that President Harry S. Truman's administration gave military aid to France in its colonial war against the communist-led Viet Minh, thus directly involving the United States in Vietnam; that in 1954 President Dwight D. Eisenhower decided to prevent a communist takeover of South Vietnam and to undermine the new communist regime of North Vietnam; that President John F. Kennedy transformed the policy of "limited-risk gamble" that he had inherited into a policy of "broad commitment"; that President Lyndon B. Johnson intensified covert warfare against North Vietnam and began planning to wage overt war in 1964, a full year before the depth of U.S. involvement was publicly revealed; and that Johnson ordered the bombing of North Vietnam in 1965 despite the judgment of the U.S. intelligence community that it would not cause the North Vietnamese to cease their support of the Viet Cong insurgency in South Vietnam.

The release of the Pentagon Papers stirred nationwide and, indeed, international controversy because it occurred after several years of growing dissent over the legal and moral justification of intensifying U.S. actions in Vietnam. The disclosures and their con-

Members of the *New York Times* composing room look at a proof sheet of a page containing the once-secret Pentagon Papers in New York, June 30, 1971.

TEXAS V. JOHNSON

Most uses of language, whether written or spoken, are clearly understood to be speech. But what about a symbolic act, such as burning a national flag as an expression of protest? In its controversial *Texas* v. *Johnson* decision, issued on June 21, 1989, the U.S. Supreme Court ruled that the burning of the U.S. flag was a constitutionally protected form of speech under the U.S. Constitution's First Amendment.

The case originated during the Republican National Convention in Dallas in August 1984, when the party had gathered to nominate President Ronald Reagan as its candidate in that year's presidential election. Gregory Lee Johnson, part of a group that had gathered to protest Reagan's policies, doused an American flag with kerosene and lit it on fire in front of the Dallas City Hall. He was arrested for violating Texas's state law that prohibited desecration of the U.S. flag and eventually was convicted; he was fined and sentenced to one year in jail. His conviction subsequently was overturned by the Texas Court of Criminal Appeals (the state's highest appeals court for criminal cases), which argued that symbolic speech was protected by the First Amendment.

The case was accepted for review by the U.S. Supreme Court, and oral arguments were heard in March 1989. In June, the Supreme Court

U.S. President Ronald Reagan (*left*) and Vice President George H. W. Bush wave to supporters at the 1984 Republican National Convention in Dallas, Texas.

released a controversial 5–4 ruling in which it upheld the appeals court decision that desecration of the U.S. flag was constitutionally protected, calling the First Amendment's protection of speech a "bedrock principle" and stating that the government could not prohibit "expression of an idea simply because society finds the idea itself offensive or disagreeable." Justice William J. Brennan, Jr., noted for his liberal jurisprudence, wrote the majority opinion and was joined by fellow liberals Thurgood Marshall and Harry Blackmun, as well as by conservatives Anthony Kennedy and Antonin Scalia.

tinued publication despite top-secret classification were embarrassing to the administration of President Richard M. Nixon, who was preparing to seek reelection in 1972. So distressing were these revelations that Nixon authorized unlawful efforts to discredit Ellsberg, efforts that came to light during the investigation of the Watergate scandal. The papers were subsequently published in book form as *The Pentagon Papers* (1971).

BURWELL V. HOBBY LOBBY STORES, INC.

In *Burwell* v. *Hobby Lobby*, Inc. (2014), the Supreme Court held (5–4) that the Religious Freedom Restoration Act (RFRA) of 1993 permits for-profit corporations that are closely held (e.g., owned by a family or family trust) to refuse, on religious grounds, to pay for legally mandated coverage of certain contraceptive drugs and devices in their employees' health insurance plans. In so ruling, the court embraced the view that closely held for-profit corporations are legal "persons" under the RFRA and are therefore capable of exercising religion.

David and Barbara Green, their children, and the for-profit corporations they owned—Hobby Lobby, Inc. (an arts-and-crafts retailer) and Mardel Christian & Education Stores, Inc. (a chain of Christian bookstores)—were the plaintiffs. They alleged that the imminent enforcement of a regulation issued by the U.S. Department of Health and

Human Services (HHS) pursuant to the Patient Protection and Affordable Care Act (2010) would infringe their rights under the RFRA. The Greens also contended that the regulation would violate the free-exercise clause of the First Amendment.

Eventually known as the contraceptive mandate, the regulation required companies with 50 or more employees to provide insurance coverage of the 20 contraceptive methods then approved by the Food and Drug Administration (FDA). Despite scientific consensus to the contrary, the Greens believed that four of those methods—two types of "morning after" pills and two types of intrauterine devices (IUDs)—were abortifacients (abortion inducers). On that basis they also believed that providing coverage of those methods in their employees' health insurance plans would be tantamount to facilitating abortion and therefore inconsistent with the tenets of their Christian faith.

The court took care to caution that its decision concerned only the lawfulness of the contraceptive mandate and should not be understood to imply that any insurance-coverage mandate (e.g., for transfusions or immunizations) "must necessarily fall if it conflicts with an employer's religious beliefs." The court also denied that its decision might enable an employer to cloak racial discrimination in hiring as a religious practice.

CONCLUSION

Despite the declaration of free states in 1776, the U.S. Constitution—the establishment of the union and its laws, as we know it—was not formulated until the Constitutional Convention (1787). This has formed the basis and touchstone for the government of the United States of America that has lasted for over 200 years. It was preceded by the Articles of Confederation.

Stimulated by severe economic troubles that produced radical political movements and urged on by a demand for a stronger central government, the convention met in the Pennsylvania State House in Philadelphia (May 25–September 17, 1787), ostensibly to amend the Articles of Confederation. All the states except Rhode Island responded to the invitation issued by the Annapolis Convention of 1786 to send delegates. Of the 74 deputies chosen by the state legislatures, only 55 took part in the proceedings; of these, 39 signed the Constitution. None could have known how long the results of their work would be upheld or predict the subjects of the amendments that would be tacked onto it over the coming decades.

Rather than amending the existing Articles of Confederation, the assembly in 1787 set about drawing up a new scheme of government. Opinion was divided—delegates from small states (without claims to unoccupied western lands) opposed those from large states over the apportionment of representation. The large state plan provided for a bicameral legislature with representation of each state based on its population or wealth. A small state plan provided for equal representation in Congress. But neither the large nor the small states would yield. Oliver Ellsworth and Roger Sherman, among others, formulated what is known as the Great Compromise: a bicameral legislature with proportional representation in the lower house and equal representation of the states in the upper house. All revenue measures would originate in the lower house. That compromise was approved on July 16. Thirty-nine members signed the final draft of the Constitution on September 17, 1787, a day now celebrated as Constitution Day.

GLOSSARY

ADJUDICATION A formal judgement on a disputed matter.

BICAMERAL Having, consisting of, or based on two legislative chambers.

COMPROMISE Settlement of differences by arbitration or by consent reached by mutual concessions.

CONFEDERATION A group of people, countries, organizations, etc., that are joined together in some activity or effort.

CONSTITUTION The basic principles and laws of a nation, state, or social group that determine the powers and duties of the government and guarantee certain rights to the people in it; a written instrument embodying the rules of a political or social organization.

DELEGATE A person acting for another, such as a representative to a convention or conference.

DEMOCRACY A government in which the supreme power is vested in the people and exercised by them directly or indirectly through a system of representation usually involving periodically held free elections.

FRANCHISE A constitutional or statutory right or privilege, especially the right to vote.

INHERENT Involved in the constitution or essential character of something; belonging by nature or habit; intrinsic.

MEDIATION Intervention between conflicting parties to promote reconciliation, settlement, or compromise.

MILITANT Aggressively active (as in a cause); combative.

NATIONALISM A movement or government advocating for national independence or a strong national government.

NULLIFICATION In the United States, the action of a state impeding or attempting to prevent the operation and enforcement within its territory of a federal law.

OMBUDSMAN A government official appointed to receive and investigate complaints made by individuals against abuses or capricious acts of public officials.

RADICALISM The quality or state of being associated with political views, practices, and policies of extreme change; advocating extreme measures to retain or restore a political state of affairs.

RATIFICATION The act or process of approving and formally sanctioning something (such as a treaty or amendment).

REPUBLIC A government in which supreme power resides in a body of citizens entitled to vote and is exercised by elected officers and representatives responsible to them and governing according to law; a political unit (such as a nation) having such a form of government.

SCHEME A plan or program of action.

SECULAR Of, relating to, or controlled by the government or the people rather than by the church.

SUBSTANTIVE Considerable in amount or numbers; creating and defining rights and duties.

TERRITORIES A geographic area belonging to or under the jurisdiction of a governmental authority; a part of the United States not included within any state but organized with a separate legislature.

TREASON The offense of attempting by overt acts to overthrow the government of the state to which the offender owes allegiance or to kill or personally injure the sovereign or the sovereign's family.

TREATISE A systematic exposition or argument in writing including a methodical discussion of the facts and principles involved and conclusions reached.

BIBLIOGRAPHY

U.S. CONSTITUTION

Cass R. Sunstein, *The Declaration of Independence and the Constitution of the United States of America* (2003), contains the full texts of the documents and a useful preface. A concise introduction is Erin Ackerman and Benjamin Ginsberg, *A Guide to the United States Constitution*, 3rd ed. (2015). John R. Vile, *A Companion to the United States Constitution and Its Amendments*, 5th ed. (2010), is a comprehensive reference work.

Catherine Drinker Bowen, *Miracle at Philadelphia* (1966, reissued 1986), examines the debates in and the events surrounding the Constitutional Convention. Books focusing on the origins of the Constitution and the intentions of its framers include Carol Berkin, *A Brilliant Solution: Inventing the American Constitution* (2002); Forrest McDonald, *Novus Ordo Seclorum: The Intellectual Origins of the Constitution* (1985); Jack N. Rakove, *Original Meanings: Politics and Ideas in the Making of the Constitution* (1996); and David Brian Robertson, *The Original Compromise: What the Constitution's Framers Were Really Thinking* (2013). Charles A. Beard, *An Economic Interpretation of the Constitution of the United States* (1913, reissued 2004), is a critical analysis of the motives of the framers.

THE FEDERALIST PAPERS

Hamilton's public and private life is examined in Nathan Schachner, *Alexander Hamilton* (1946, reissued 1961), well-balanced and readable; Broadus Mitchell, *Alexander Hamilton*, 2 vol. (1957–62), a scholarly study; and John Chester Miller, *Alexander Hamilton and the Growth of the New Nation* (2004; originally published as *Alexander Hamilton: Portrait in Paradox*, 1959), strong on his public career. Harvey Flaumenhaft, *The Effective Republic: Administration and Constitution in the Thought of Alexander Hamilton* (1992); and Forrest McDonald, *Alexander Hamilton*, collector's ed. (1995), reexamine his political philosophy. Other biographies include Jacob Ernest Cooke, *Alexander Hamilton* (1982); Marie B. Hecht, *Odd Destiny: The Life of Alexander Hamilton* (1982); Richard Brookhiser, *Alexander Hamilton, American* (1999); and Ron Chernow, *Alexander Hamilton* (2004). John Sedgwick, *War of Two: Alexander Hamilton, Aaron Burr, and the Duel That Stunned the Nation* (2015) studies the duel that ended Hamilton's life. Douglas Ambrose and Robert W.T. Martin (eds.), *The Many Faces of Alexander Hamilton: The Life and Legacy of America's Most Elusive Founding Father* (2006), is a collection of essays by leading Hamilton scholars.

Frank Monaghan, *John Jay* (1935, reissued 1972), is a well-written biography. Richard B. Morris, *Witnesses at the Creation: Hamilton, Madison, Jay, and the Constitution* (1985), characterizes the three men and analyzes the events surrounding the writing of the Federalist Papers.

William T. Hutchinson et al. (eds.), *The Papers of James Madison*, 17 vol. (1962–91), is the most extensive collection of Madison's writings, annotated and with background notes. Gaillard Hunt (ed.), *The Writings of James Madison*, 9 vol. (1900–10), comprises Madison's public papers and private correspondence, and Hunt also edited *The Journal of the Debates in the Convention Which Framed the Constitution of the United States, May–September 1787, As Recorded by James Madison*, 2 vol. (1908), which is the only continuous and an almost exhaustive record of that convention. James Morton Smith (ed.), *The Republic of Letters: The Correspondence Between Thomas Jefferson and James Madison, 1776–1826*, 3 vol. (1995), includes more than 1,200 letters detailing their friendship. A valuable briefer presentation of this subject is Adrienne Koch, *Jefferson and Madison: The Great Collaboration* (1950, reprinted 1987).

Madison's life is most competently and exhaustively treated by Irving Brant, *James Madison*, 6 vol. (1941–61), which sets out to counter the hitherto prevailing misrepresentation of the Madison and Jefferson administrations and particularly the derogation of Madison relative to Jefferson; Brant's *The Fourth President* (1970) selectively condenses the multivolume work into a single volume. Ralph Ketcham, *James Madison* (1971, reprinted 1990), is also good. Drew R. McCoy, *The Last of the Fathers: James Madison and the Republican Legacy* (1989), tells about the man after his presidential career.

The following works discuss and evaluate Madison's political career and administrations: the first section of John Quincy Adams, *The Lives of James Madison and James Monroe*,

Fourth and Fifth Presidents of the United States (1850); William C. Rives, *History of the Life and Times of James Madison*, 3 vol. (1859–68, reprinted 1970), concentrating on the period from the American Revolution until 1797; Sydney Howard Gay, *James Madison* (1884, reissued 1983), covering up to 1797; William Lee Miller, *The Business of May Next: James Madison and the Founding* (1992), detailing the period from 1784 to 1791; and Robert Allen Rutland, *The Presidency of James Madison* (1990), focusing on the War of 1812.

Madison's political philosophy is analyzed in Stuart G. Brown, *The First Republicans: Political Philosophy and Public Policy in the Party of Jefferson and Madison* (1954, reprinted 1976), a work concerned with Madison, Monroe, and Jefferson and the development of the essential partisan ideas that bound together the republican faction; Irving Brant, *James Madison and American Nationalism* (1968), an account of Madison's role in the formation and development of U.S. institutions against the background of the popular attitude, with corroboratory documentary readings; Lance Banning, *The Sacred Fire of Liberty: James Madison and the Founding of the Federal Republic* (1995), explaining Madison's views on national government; and Richard K. Matthews, *If Men Were Angels: James Madison and the Heartless Empire of Reason* (1995), contending that Madison followed liberal political beliefs.

INDEX